Merry Ex-Mas

Victoria Christopher Murray

Other Works by Victoria Christopher Murray

Jasmine Series
Temptation
A Sin and a Shame
Too Little, Too Late
Lady Jasmine
Sins of the Mother
Scandalous

**Co-Written with
ReShonda Tate Billingsley**
Sinners & Saints
Friends & Foes

Single Titles
Joy
Blessed Assurance
Truth Be Told
Grown Folks Business
The Ex Files
The Deal, the Dance, and the Devil
Destiny's Divas
Never Say Never

**The Divas Series
(teen fiction)**
Diamond
India
Veronique
Aaliyah

One

Sheridan Hart Goodman

"Boy, do you know how many hours I labored just to give you life!" Although I had asked my son that question before, with what he was asking me to do, I needed to remind him. "I pushed and pulled and screamed for twenty-three hours, seven minutes, and sixty-three seconds."

Leaning against the dresser, my son, Christopher, laughed the way he always did when I went into this rant. "Ma, why do you say sixty-three seconds? Just add another minute—make it eight minutes and three seconds."

I waved my finger in Christopher's face. "My math is not the issue here. The issue is that you're asking me to go above and beyond being the wonderful mother that I already am."

"Yes, you are." Christopher slung his arm over my shoulder, and I knew that was another trick. "You have been the best mother ever," he said, laying the butter on thick. "But I just need you to take it up a notch. Just this one time. Just this one little thing."

"Trust me, what you're asking me to do is no little thing."

"But it's important to me," Christopher said.

"Why?" I whined. I knew I sounded like a child, so I figured I'd go all the way. I twisted away from Christopher, plopped down on the edge of my bed, folded my arms, and pouted.

Christopher laughed as he crossed the room, then gently eased down next to me. In a tone that was full of patience, he said, "I told you, Ma. I really want Evon's first Christmas with our family to be special." Then he softened his voice and added, "Don't you?"

Foul! I wanted to yell at him. This was emotional blackmail. I should know—I was a mother and used it often.

"That's what you want, right?" Christopher asked. "A special Christmas for me and my wife-to-be?"

With every word, my son was breaking me down just a little bit more...and he knew it!

"Evon and me." Christopher said his fiancée's name again, knowing that I adored the young woman that he'd chosen to marry.

My lips betrayed me; I couldn't help it—I smiled. Of course I wanted this Christmas to be wonderful. This was the beginning of a whole new life for us. In six months, my baby boy, my son, my Christopher was going to be a husband. That, by itself, was hard enough to believe. And that meant I was going to be a mother-in-law. And I was going to be a wonderful one because Christopher had chosen well.

Suddenly, Kem's voice filled my bedroom. *"If it's love, it'll last a lifetime...."* Christopher unhooked his cell from his holster, but he was grinning before he even looked down at the screen. "Ma, I gotta take this," he said, trotting out of the room.

He didn't even give me a chance to tell him that it was okay and that I was glad that Evon had chosen this very minute to call. Maybe by the time he hung up, he would've forgotten what he was asking me to do.

I couldn't believe Christopher actually wanted me to invite his father to Christmas dinner.

His father, my ex-husband, who in 2004 had sent our entire family into turmoil and, at the same time, had almost ruined Christopher's life. Losing Quentin, the man I'd been married to for seventeen years, the man who was the love of my life, was bad enough; but what that breakup did to our sixteen-year-old son? It was crazy.

It all started the day that Quentin had announced to the world that he'd been playing for the wrong team—that he was gay. From that day, Christopher had done everything in his power to prove that he was nothing like his father. My son had searched far outside his Jack and Jill circle and found Deja, the first girl that he'd ever brought home for me to meet.

Deja Blue, the youngest of seven girls, was raised by a single father who'd taught his daughters that more important than education was finding boys who could take care of them. Thank

God, Deja had been nothing more than a high school, first-lust, first-sex, get-back-at-my-father fling.

Deja may have been the first, but Evon LaCroix was the last and she was the real deal. I just loved that young woman, whose face always shone brighter than the sun. I'm telling you, I would bet that not a tear had ever been shed out of her twinkling brown eyes. Just being around her made me happy.

All of that alone would have been good enough for me, but the bonus was that Evon was sharp, mentally and physically. She was a Harvard grad who was born with a strong fashion sense, and she planned to put her education to use as a fashion entrepreneur with her LaCroix Designs. So yes, I wanted her to have a great Christmas with us, but did having Quentin here have to be part of the deal?

"So, Ma," Christopher said, strutting back into the bedroom.

Just the way he said that, I knew he wanted to pick the conversation up right where we'd left off.

He continued, "All I'm trying to do is show Evon how we do it. I want her to see the wonderful Christmases that we have and how it's gonna be for her when she becomes a Hart."

"I agree. And she'll see all of that. It's not necessary to bring your father into this. You haven't spent Christmas with him in what? Over eight years?" I shook my head. "No, we don't need him here for Christmas."

Then Christopher lowered his eyes and glanced up at me through his eyelashes. "Please," he whispered.

I used to think that was so cute, and it would've helped him— if this were eight years ago. Because Christopher looking at me like that—that was all Quentin. And looking and sounding like his father right now was not a winning strategy.

"No, Christopher. I'm not inviting your father."

"Come on, Ma!"

"And think about it...what would Brock say?"

"What would Brock say about what?" my husband said as he stepped into our bedroom.

I jumped up and wrapped my arms around the finest man that I knew. "Hey, honey, I didn't hear you come in."

"That's because you were too busy saying no to me," Christopher said.

My husband looked at me and then switched to Christopher. "What's going on?"

"Christopher is *trying* to talk me into something, and I'm not having it."

Brock turned to Christopher. "You haven't convinced her about your father?"

That made me blink over and over. "You know what Christopher wants me to do?"

Brock nodded, but it was Christopher who spoke up. "Yeah, Ma. I talked to him last night. I wasn't going to disrespect Brock by going to you first."

"Oh, so just disrespect me."

"You know that's not what I meant." Then he shrugged. "It's just that Brock's the man of the house, and I understand these man things. I wanted to give him his props, his due respect. And I knew you'd understand that."

I started grinning hard. How could I be mad at that? But then I remembered what Christopher wanted me to do, and I snatched my smile back. "So you guys talked and..."

Brock put his arms around me like he thought he'd better be holding me when he said, "I told him I thought it was a good idea."

I wiggled away from him. "Traitor!"

He laughed. "Ah, come on; we're all grown up now," Brock said as he pulled me back to him. "First of all, I won; you're my bride."

I loved when he said that, when he called me his bride, even though we'd been married for six years.

He added, "So I don't have any beef with Quentin. Plus, Christopher wants to show off his family to Evon. He wants her to really see that he comes from good stock."

"She knows that already. She's met me and you."

"And she's met Dad, too, obviously," Christopher piped in, "but now, she'll get to see all of us together."

"Yeah," Brock said, "she'll get to see the cohesive blended family that we are."

I rolled my eyes. It sounded good, but the reality of it—sitting down with Quentin and whatever man he was with...I shuddered. Looking up at Brock, I said, "I've known you for nine years, and now you turn on me?"

He laughed, but I didn't find a single thing funny.

"You know I love me some you," he said. "But baby, this isn't about us. This is about our children, this family, and this Christmas."

Game over! Because Brock had me whenever he referred to Christopher and Tori as his children. That's how he'd always been. From the moment when I'd finally introduced my son and daughter to him, Brock had thought of Christopher and Tori as his own.

I still remembered the conversation he had when we told the kids that we were getting married. "You two already have a father, and I'm not trying to replace him. But I want you to know that I love you because I love your mother. And I'll always be here for you in whatever way that you need me."

Right after that, he'd asked their permission to marry me, and it had been a love fest all around since then.

Brock said, "So, we're all having Christmas dinner...here...together...as a family?"

I was almost ready to say yes, but I still had to give it one more try. Glancing at Christopher, I said, "I thought you didn't want to have anything to do with your father?"

Christopher frowned as if he was trying to figure out what I was talking about. "Are you talking about when I was sixteen?"

I nodded. "Can't we go back to those days?"

"Ma!"

"Sheridan!"

Brock and Christopher shouted at me at the same time. Then Brock added, "Can't we just do this for our son?"

There it was again. Our son. The way he had pulled my children into his heart, how could I say no?

I nodded, though I barely moved my head. I didn't want either one of them to think that they'd totally won me over. I didn't want them to think that I totally agreed because I knew something they didn't know. I couldn't explain it, but it was in my gut—eating turkey with Quentin and his man on Christmas was sure to be a disaster.

"Yes!" Christopher pumped his fist in the air. "Thank you!" He kissed my cheek and then bumped fists with Brock. "Thanks, dude!"

"You got it 'cause I'm just trying to help you out; I'm just making sure that Evon doesn't give you back that big ole ring that she's rockin'."

Christopher laughed one more time before he kissed me again, and then he strutted out of the room like he'd just won the current forty-million-dollar Powerball.

Brock followed him to the door, then closed it behind him. When he turned back to me, I shook my head. "What was up with that? I thought you didn't like my ex?"

"I told you—I don't have a problem with Quentin. Once I put that ring on your finger, he became my best friend. Because of him, I have you. How can I hate on that?"

He kissed my neck, and inside I moaned. But I wasn't ready to give in totally...yet. "You're just trying to butter me up so that I'll do this."

He laughed. "No, 'cause you already agreed. It's a done deal, and we're gonna have fun doing it."

"Dinner with Quentin and whatever man he's seeing now? Yeah, it's gonna be a real Christmas day at the beach." I sighed. "Do you really think I can do this?"

He nodded. "Yes, 'cause you're my beautiful, wonderful, amazing wife and you can do anything." Then when he pressed his plump lips against mine, that tingling began in the soles of my feet and began rising, rising.

But even when he pushed me back onto the bed and lay on top of me, I couldn't stop the thoughts in my head. I was really going to have Christmas dinner with Quentin Hart. Christmas with my ex. This was going to take a lot of prayer.

Oh joy, joy, joy!

Joy to the world!

Two

Kendall Leigh Stewart

$\mathcal{F}$rom the moment I got the call from my father this morning, I knew exactly what he wanted. This was our annual pre-Christmas caucus. This was when he'd beg me to come to Christmas dinner, and I'd have to tell him what I'd told him for the last six years: No!

I sighed as I peeked through the windshield at my Compton childhood home. Why did my father put himself through this? By now, he should have gotten the message; I was never going to change my mind. I wished that he would just stop asking. For him and for me. Because every time my father called right before Christmas, he reminded me. And I was taken back to the day when this started all those years ago...

I couldn't wait to get home. Anthony and I had been so off-kilter for the last few months, and I wanted to do something about that. Especially with the way I'd left for San Francisco yesterday morning. I still felt bad about the special night that Anthony had prepared for me—a celebration the night before I left for this business trip. But the thing was, I didn't know about his plans. And once he'd told me, it was too late for me to change mine. I had planned another long, long night at the office. This meeting with the Ozark people in San Fran was too important for me not to be totally prepared. I really wanted their specialty products in our spa, and I needed to put the final touches on my presentation.

Of course, because I wouldn't change my plans, it had turned into just another one of the thousands of blowups I had with my husband. Anthony accused me of always putting work ahead of him, and I told him that I thought I'd married a grown man and not a whiny boy.

The look in his eyes when I said that made me want to snatch those words back. Made me try a different approach.

"This is all for our future," I tried to convince him.

But though my approach was different, his wasn't. "If you keep this up, we may never have a future."

His words had shocked me. "What does that mean?"

He didn't answer, just stomped away.

It felt like a tantrum to me, and I didn't have time to handle it then, but I planned on handling it now. Tonight. In our bedroom. In our bed.

Just me coming home early from this business trip—something that I'd never done before—would prove to Anthony that I was serious about us and our marriage. I knew I wasn't good at this wife thing. Maybe it was because, as a little girl, I'd never wanted to grow up to be a wife. Maybe it was because I saw Anthony as more of my business partner than my husband. But whatever my issues were, I wanted to get it right, now. I'd probably need some counseling, and I was fine with that.

I'd start with tonight, though. Just me and Anthony.

It was just about five minutes before a new day when the cab eased to the side of the road on PCH and stopped at our home. Every time I pulled up in front of our Malibu beachside house, I was reminded of just how blessed I was. And I was going to not only tell my husband that tonight, I was going to show him.

I rushed through the front door and dropped my bag right at the entry. Of course, the house was dark, but not pitch-black since the midnight moon that lit the beach seeped through the living room's magnificent glass wall. As I headed up the stairs, I was already peeling off my clothes, getting ready for my husband.

And then I got to the doorway of our bedroom.

And I stopped.

I was frozen, but only for a moment.

Truly, my eyes had to be deceiving me. It was dark, so my brain had confused my eyes because I couldn't be seeing what I saw. That's why I turned on the light. The bright overhead light that lit up the bedroom like the shining sun. The light we never used because it was so bright. But the light that I needed now.

Anthony was home. In bed. But he was not alone.

I screamed.

And then he screamed. And then she screamed.

"Oh, my god!"

I think I was the one who said that because the next thing I heard was, "Kendall!"

That was Anthony, but I couldn't concentrate on him. Because my eyes wouldn't move from the woman who held the sheet, my sheet, from my bed, over her bare chest.

"Kendall!" Anthony yelled my name again.

It wasn't until he touched me that I was finally freed from my catatonic state. That was when I stumbled out of the bedroom and staggered down the stairs. Thick tears clouded my eyes, slowing me down as I struggled to open the garage door and jump into my car.

I was surprised that Anthony hadn't caught up to me, but I guess I had an advantage—I was already dressed.

The tires screamed as I shifted the car into reverse and pressed the accelerator to the floor. Then I pushed the car into drive and did the same thing. I drove, with no destination in mind, but after only a few minutes, I couldn't keep going. I was truly blinded by my tears and wouldn't make it much further. But where was I going to go?

It didn't take me long to figure that out, nor long to get there. But if I'd been thinking straight, I would've chosen someplace else. Because five minutes after I arrived in my office, Anthony barreled in.

"Kendall!" There was relief in his voice. "Oh, my god!"

I turned to face him and the way he looked at me, I wondered what he saw. I knew he could see my swollen, red eyes, but could he see my busted heart, too? That's the part that I wanted him to see. I wanted to rip my blouse open, slash my skin, and show him my heart that I knew would never, ever be the same.

But with all of that in my mind, the only words that came out of me were, "How could you?"

He shook his head slowly, and that's when I noticed that his eyes were as puffed up as mine. I wondered why—it wasn't like he had any reason to hurt.

"Kendall," he said, "I'm so sorry."

But I didn't want to hear any apologies. I just wanted my answer. "How could you?" I asked him again through my sobs.

There was nothing but sorrow in his eyes, and I wanted to smack that out of him. "I'm sorry," he kept saying. "We can try to work through this...it was just this one time."

One time? So that was supposed to make a difference?

He said, "Please, Kendall. Please, let's try."

I said, "Why...why Sabrina? Why my sister?"

I had to do what I always did when I tortured myself with that memory. I squeezed my eyes shut and tried to push all of that to the back of my mind.

But the memory was never far enough away. It stayed close enough to come back. Especially at Christmas when my father summoned me. For this talk.

It was only because I loved and respected him that I came when he called.

Pushing open the car door, I inhaled a deep breath of courage, then trotted up the three steps before I put my key in the front door. Before I turned the lock, I said a quick prayer asking God to make this short because I knew it wasn't going to be sweet.

"Daddy!" I yelled out the moment I stepped inside. "I'm here."

The sound of Michael Jackson's pre-teen voice played through the speakers in the living room.

Santa Claus is coming to town....

I laughed out loud at the song that brought back so many memories. What was going on? I paused right at the door as I took in the sight in front of me with wonder. I'd just been here on Tuesday, but in the four days since we'd had our regular weekly dinner together, my father had turned his home into "Christmas Present."

From the time we were little kids, Dad always tried to get the biggest tree with the brightest lights. But this year, he'd done even more. Besides the six-foot tree that stood in front of the bay window, garland was draped across the four walls of the living room, and he'd even hung red felt stockings on the fireplace exactly the way he used to do when we were kids.

But it was the mistletoe swinging above the entryway between the living room and the kitchen that made me laugh out loud. Who had my dad been kissing? Now, I had a few questions for him, but whatever was going on, I wasn't going to be mad. Whatever it was that was making him fill his house with all of this cheer was all right with me.

"Baby girl? Is that you?"

My father had the kind of voice that I could listen to all night—whether he was talking or singing, it was always melodic. It always made me smile.

But then, I heard the slow, soft shuffles of his slippers sliding along the parquet hallway floor, and my smile faded quickly. He didn't move the way he used to, and the sound made me remember that my father was truly getting older.

When he appeared at the edge of the living room, I tried not to frown. Now, I'd just seen my father on Tuesday, and though I thought he'd lost a little weight then, I could really see it now. It was the way his bathrobe hung from his frame--like it was a size too big. And his shoulders were a little hunched over. That wasn't like him; he always stood so tall, so proud.

But I wasn't going to let him see any of my concern. "Hey, Daddy."

"Baby girl." First in the way he called me that and then in the way he hugged me, I had no doubt that my father truly loved me.

When my arms tightened around him, I could really feel his thinness. How much weight had he lost? And why was I just noticing that? Stepping back from his embrace, I asked, "How you doing, Daddy?"

He smiled, nodded. "I'm good."

"You seem like you've lost a little weight." I did my best to keep my concern out of my voice. "It must be all the working out you've been doing." I chuckled a little just to keep it light. But I really did want to know what was going on.

"Yeah, you know I love that elliptical thing that you got for me. I try to do it every day." He motioned toward the sofa. "Let's sit down."

I followed behind him and tried to do a measurement in my mind. My father was six-three, but right now, he didn't look close to six feet. Was he shrinking?

"I'm thinking maybe you're working out too much," I said. "Maybe you don't need to do it every day. You might need a day of rest."

He shook his head. "I don't have time to slow down, honey," he said as he sat in the chair across from me. "I'm an old man; I gotta do as much as I can right now."

I waved my hand like his words didn't mean anything. "You're not hardly old. Seventy-one is the new fifty-one."

That made him laugh out loud. "Well somebody needs to tell these old bones 'cause they don't know that they're twenty years younger."

"Whatever, you're not old!" I said it like those words were a demand. I wanted him to believe what I was telling him.

"How you doin', baby girl?" he asked, changing the subject. "Business good?"

"Yeah." This was a question that he asked me every time we got together.

And then he said, "Kendall," in that special way that meant that some serious business was about to be discussed. In that moment, I remembered—because I had surely forgotten—why my father had summoned me here.

Remembering now made me tense up, made me press my hands into my lap and try to hide the way my fingers had curled into fists.

"It's almost Christmas," my father said as if that were a news flash. "And then came the punch line. "I want us all to have Christmas dinner together this year."

It was amazing to me that my father's words hadn't changed since 2007. But then, I never changed my word either. "No!" That was it. That was simple. That's the way it was.

It was like my father didn't hear my "No!" He said, "You know how you've had dreams and gone after them your whole life, baby girl?" He stopped, turned and focused his eyes on the photos that crowded the mantel.

My father had just changed up the script, and that made me frown. This wasn't part of our normal talk.

He said, "Well, I have dreams, too," and turned back to face me. "This year, my greatest dream is that we all sit down at the table right there," he paused and pointed to the dining room table behind him, "and have Christmas dinner."

I pressed my lips together. I was really proud of myself; I'd gotten so much better at swallowing the first words that came to my mind—at least with my father. Six years ago, when he had invited me to that first dinner after Anthony and Sabrina's betrayal, I had jumped up and down, wailing the whole time. I shouted, I screamed, and then I stomped out of the house, completely insulted that my father had asked me to break bread with the likes of my sister.

But even though those emotions still rumbled inside of me, I kept my rage to myself.

Make no mistake, though, the years hadn't softened my heart. Every single time my father brought up Christmas, it made me think of the two people that I had once loved the most, but who now topped my enemies list.

But what woman wouldn't feel bad about: One—her sister sleeping with her husband. Two—her husband then leaving her. And three—her husband then marrying her sister.

Not that it had completely happened that way. I mean, Anthony did apologize and beg and apologize some more. He begged me to come back. He kept explaining that it had only happened one time. I kept telling him that one time was my threshold.

"I really want this," my father pushed through my thoughts. "We're a family, Kendall. No matter what. You, me...Sabrina and Anthony."

I exhaled. Their names passed through my mind but never passed through my lips. And it was just as hard to hear them out loud. But my father had just spoken them, and I was still alive. The dagger that I felt in my heart every time I heard my sister's name hadn't twisted and taken my life away from me.

"And," my father kept talking, "of course, you could bring anyone with you that you want."

Now, my father knew that I wasn't seeing a soul. All of my time was invested in my business; that was my life. Plus after what had happened with Anthony...and even what had gone down with my mother and father, a good relationship wasn't part of my DNA.

I shook my head, and though I smiled, my father got my message.

He released a small sigh. "I know how much you've been hurt, baby girl," he said, going right back to my pain. "I know how awful it was then, and I know the years haven't done much to soften your heart. But it's my dream. My dream..." He left it at that.

On the drive over, I had planned all the words that I was going to say. The same words that would break his heart all over again. "Daddy, you know, I appreciate and understand everything that you're saying...." Then I pushed out my final words on this subject, "But, I'm sorry, you're going to have to give me a little more time."

My dad nodded as if those were exactly the words he expected. "Time," he whispered. "A little more time."

He made me frown again. This was the second time that my dad had deviated from our normal conversation. This was the point in the conversation when he was supposed to tell me that it was time to let it go so that I could heal. He was supposed to remind me how Sabrina and Anthony had tried to do right, and how even after I set our divorce in motion, the two had stayed away from each other. He was supposed to convince me that my sister and my ex-husband had given it a heroic try, but the two really were destined to be together.

But my father didn't say any of those things. Something was different. Something felt wrong.

When he stood and moved to the ottoman right in front of me, I knew for sure that something was up. By the time he reached for my hands, my heart was pounding.

"This is not just about Christmas, baby girl," he said, looking straight into my eyes without even blinking.

"What's going on?"

"I don't want to drag this out, so..." He inhaled as if he needed extra air to keep going. "I want us to have Christmas together because of what you said. Because of time...and I don't know how much time I have left."

That was when the pace of my heart steadied, and I laughed, relieved. For a moment, I thought something was really wrong, but my dad was just being dramatic—though, that was not like him. "Oh, Daddy." I swatted the air like I was shooing his words away. "You're fine. You'll probably outlive me."

He chuckled, though there was more bitter than sweet in the sound. He squeezed my hands, tighter now. "I *have* lived a mighty good life."

Okay, my heart started pumping again, because now his words, his tone sounded like a eulogy.

"Daddy..."

"Whew! This is harder for me to say than I thought." He looked down, then back up again. "I'm dying, Kendall. The doctors tell me that I don't have long to live."

Between the time my dad's words left his lips and reached my ears, something had happened. Because surely, the words were jumbled. That was the only explanation I had for hearing, "I don't have long to live."

He couldn't have said that because those words could never be true. There was no way that I could live the rest of my life without my father when I'd already been cheated out of years with my mother.

"Kendall?" my father called me.

I tried to open my mouth to question my dad, ask him what in the heavens was he talking about. But there was something wrong—my lips wouldn't move.

"Baby girl, say something, please!"

I wanted to speak because there were a million questions I wanted to ask and a million assurances that I wanted to give.

And then there was the big thing that I really wanted to say. I wanted to demand that my father not die because I'd never be able to breathe without him.

"Say something," my father told me again.

I wanted to obey him, I really did. But my tongue became thick, and my lips were paralyzed. So I did the only thing that I could do.

I burst into tears. And I cried, while through the speakers, Mary J. Blige sang, *And have yourself a merry little Christmas now....*

That was my all-time favorite Christmas song by one of my all-time favorite singers. But I would never want to hear that song again. Not ever.

Three

Asia Ingrum

I leaned back in the massage chair and lifted both of my feet into the air.

"Do you like it, Ms. Asia?"

I shifted my toes to the left, then the right. The gold polish that was sprinkled with glitter made my toenails glisten as if they were covered with diamonds. Oh, this was all the way good; my feet looked like they were worth a hundred thousand dollars—each.

"I love this, Susie," I said to the nail technician who was always on call for me. All I had to do was press her number in my cell and—bam! In ten minutes flat, she'd be there. "Just fab. Perfect for Christmas."

Susie Wu gathered her supplies, rinsed the tools in the sink that I had installed in this room, and then placed them into the sterilization chamber. "Okay," Susie said when she finished, "so I'll see you next week?"

"That's the plan, but I'll call you if I need a change before New Year's Eve."

Susie shoved her purse onto her shoulder. "Well, have a merry Christmas."

"Same to you. Go on downstairs, you can let yourself out," I said. "I'm gonna sit here for a few minutes longer and make sure my toenails are really dry." I leaned back and picked up my iPad that had been resting in my lap. But before Susie was even out of the room, my eyes were closed.

This massage chair was not made for doing anything except chill-laxin', and I snuggled into the leather. It wouldn't take much longer for my toes to dry, but there was no reason for me to get up. I didn't have to rush to go anywhere; this was just another day in my extraordinary life.

I pushed a long sigh through my throat. I couldn't be anything but happy; I was in love with my life. I loved my huge condo, I loved my luxury car, and I loved my bank account balance. Not that any of this had come from working a day in my life—well, at least not working the way other people defined work. I stayed beautiful—that was my job.

"Mom!"

The scream made me sit straight up in my chair. "Dang!" I opened my eyes and looked straight into the eyes of my eleven-year-old daughter. Angel may have been a tween, but she was already five-nine, just an inch shorter than me. She was all limbs, long legs and long arms—that part she'd gotten from her father.

She'd started having these major growth spurts when she was just six, and I have to admit, I was really concerned. I mean, I wasn't worried about her height, but what would she look like with those long legs and arms that looked like they could almost drag along the ground when she walked?

But then, my daughter had this face: the best of me and Bobby. She had my almond-shaped, gray eyes and my full lips, and she had her father's thick eyebrows and dimples that were carved deep into her skin.

When I was a child, I knew I was pretty. I mean, all I had to do was look in the mirror—I'm not being conceited; that's just a fact. But here's another fact: Angel was beyond pretty. She was simply gorgeous. There was no other word to describe her.

And that was not just me talking as her mother. By the time Angel was eight years old, every agency from Elite Model Management to IMG and Ford Models was trying to make contact with Bobby Johnson's daughter. Angel had been thrilled because she'd always wanted to be a model. And an actress. And a dancer. And a singer.

I wasn't so happy about Angel pursuing modeling so young. I mean, what about just being a kid? I didn't have that privilege; I wanted her to have the real childhood that I had never had.

But Angel and Bobby had talked me into it, and Angel had signed with Ford Models. That was my concession. Their concession: Angel would only do occasional print and catalog work. I wasn't about to let my young daughter get too caught up.

"Where is the fire?" I asked her.

"Dad wants to speak to you." Angel held out her smartphone to me.

Now see, I had been feeling good, having a great day. And now my ex wanted to talk? What did Bobby Johnson want?

Not that Bobby and I didn't have a cordial relationship. I was his baby's mama...and because of that, the former all-star forward for the Los Angeles Lakers made sure that all of my needs were met. So beyond this condo, my BMW, and a bank account that came with a financial planner, I had credit cards with statements that were never mailed to my address. All of that alone made me want to be cordial to the man.

But the truth was, while I had loved him from the tips of my toes at one time, I could never forgive him for making the worst mistake of his life.

Every single moment of that morning was still etched in my mind. That morning when Bobby had come over to the condo so that we could have a special talk. That special morning, six years ago...

I had been giddy and giggling ever since Bobby called me yesterday saying we had to talk. It had been three weeks since I'd last seen him. Bobby may have just retired, but he was on the road. He'd gone back to his home in Dallas for a week, and then he had meetings all over the country, trying to decide his next move. I'd found out on the news (which pissed me off a little) that he was taking a position with ESPN L.A. But now that his professional future was set, I knew he wanted to take care of the personal side of his life.

So I had already figured out what he wanted to talk to me about—we were finally going to be a family: me, Bobby, and our baby girl.

I couldn't wait to see him; I couldn't wait to talk. And so, I made sure that I had dressed the part: a fire-red bra and thong with a matching silk knit kimono. Just as I slipped into my stiletto mules, I heard the beeps from the alarm indicating that the front door had opened.

As I came down the stairs, Bobby waited for me at the bottom, and even though we had been together for ten years, that man still made my heart do that butterfly flutter thang. Everything about that man made me go, "Hmph, hmph, hmph!" From his sculpted chest, to his bowed legs, to the way he held his head, and his lopsided smile. But the best part of him was that face. A face that every camera loved.

"Hey, baby," I whispered, pulling my voice from my throat.

As Bobby's eyes glided over me, I tossed my bone-straight hair over my shoulders and rested my hands on my waist, posing for my man. This was why I worked out; this was why I hardly ate. And this was why I was a perfect size four.

When I thought Bobby'd had his fill, I strutted over and leaned into him. I pressed against him, and I could feel the beat of his heart—and other parts. Then, Bobby did something that he never did...he eased away from me.

That made me chuckle a little. My man wasn't going to waste any time. He wanted to get right to it.

But when Bobby moved toward the living room instead of lifting me and carrying me upstairs to our bedroom, I frowned and followed him.

He faced me and said, "Asia, we need to talk."

That was when it came back to me. Seeing Bobby had almost made me forget—we were about to have *the talk*. I was giddy again and wondered if Bobby had brought the engagement ring already, or were we going to buy it together?

Bobby sat on the couch, and I eased down next to him. After he let a couple of moments pass, he said, "We've been together for a long time, and I never meant for things to go on like this for so long."

I pouted, just a little, but only because he loved it when I did that with my lips. "Baby, it's okay. The past doesn't matter. It's all about what's happening now."

His forehead creased, and that was when I realized that he really thought that I didn't know why he was here.

I laughed. "Baby, I know what you're going to say."

His frown deepened.

I said, "I knew it when you said that you wanted to come over." I cupped my hands over his. "I know this is gonna be hard, but it's best for Caroline."

Bobby flinched, but I knew why. I'd kinda broken the unspoken rule—that his wife's name was never to be spoken. But since he was about to divorce her, it didn't matter.

I said, "And this is definitely best for me and Angel."

His eyes narrowed.

I guess I just needed to come out and say it. "Angel is going to be so excited when we tell her that we're getting married."

Bobby snatched his hands away from me and jumped up like he'd been bitten by a snake. "No!" He started pacing back and forth.

"What is wrong with you, baby?" I asked him.

He was breathing heavy when he said, "You don't understand...I've decided...to stay...with my wife."

Okay, now see, I had to figure out why my man had stopped speaking English.

He said, "I'm going to be working at ESPN, and I want to change every part of my life. I want to honor my wife."

His words literally took my breath away. But I had enough air to ask, "What did you say?"

"I want to honor...my wife. I owe this to her."

That fool had gone and said the wrong thing! I sprang up from the couch and got right in his face. "Owe it to your wife? What about me? What do you owe me?"

"You'll never have to worry. I'll take care of you."

"You think that's enough?" I could feel my neck rolling with each word. I may have been living the high life for the last ten years, but right now, every bit of my Compton-life-before-Bobby was coming out of me.

"I'll take care of Angel, too."

"Damn straight since she's your daughter." I glared at him. "I cannot believe this. I thought you were coming here to tell me that we were getting married."

He looked at me as if I were the one who was speaking a different language. "I never made you that promise."

That was when I went all the way off. I reminded him that I'd had his baby. He reminded me that he had a wife. I told him that I thought he loved me. And he said nothing—just turned his back on me.

I don't know what made me do it. Maybe it was the ten years that we spent together or the fact that he was actually leaving *me* for *his wife*. But my fists started flying, hitting his face, his chest, anyplace where I could connect. It wasn't like I really thought my hands were lethal weapons, but I sure hoped that I would kill him. Or at the very least, I wanted to give him the beat down of his life.

But Bobby was stronger; he held me until I calmed down, but then he was smart enough to back out of the apartment and never take his eyes off of me....

"Mom! You've got to talk to Dad!" Angel said pushing her phone into my hand.

I blinked. It was just a couple of seconds, but with all the emotions that I'd just relived from that morning six years ago, I really didn't feel like talking to Bobby. But with Angel standing there, staring in my face, I took the phone from her.

"Be nice," she whispered.

With a tilt of my head, I painted on as fake a smile as I could. "Hello, Bobby," I said in an exaggerated, affected tone that was meant to mimic his wife's.

"Hey, Asia, what's up?" Bobby said, sounding all chipper, as if he didn't even notice what I was doing.

"Nothing," I said, returning to my own voice. "Angel said you wanted to speak to me."

"Oh, yeah." There was surprise in his tone as if he couldn't believe that I wanted to get right to business.

I understood his surprise. There were some days when I didn't feel like speaking to him, and then there were days when we would be on the phone for hours, making me sometimes feel like he was mine again. Of course, the long conversations were always under the guise of our daughter and her best interests. But when I felt like it, I could keep Bobby talking for as long as I wanted. Which was one of the reasons why I believed that I could get Bobby back if I wanted him.

Except, I didn't want him. At least, not in the way that he wanted me. If I were to ever be with Bobby, it would have to be a full-fledged relationship. All Bobby wanted, though, was a jump-off, and I was not that chick. So I'd gotten over it, over him, and had moved on.

Bobby said, "Well...uh...you know next week is Christmas."

"Yeah," I said, as I sat back in the chair and tapped in the password on my iPad. I hadn't checked my Facebook page all day, and while half-listening to Bobby, this would be the perfect time to do it.

"Well...uh..."

Okay, that made me pause. I knew Bobby Johnson. I knew him as if I were his wife. In fact, that's how he'd treated me—as his Los Angeles-based wife, while the woman who wore the real wifey ring stayed behind in their home in Dallas. So from the years when we were together, I knew everything about Bobby Johnson. I knew about the heart-shaped birthmark that was hidden inside his left thigh, I knew how he smelled after sex, and I knew how much of an attitude he had every time the Lakers lost a game. I knew his favorite cologne, his shirt size, suit size, and shoe size.

And I knew that when he stuttered, something was up.

"And uh," he stuttered.

"What is it, Bobby?" I asked. My "what's-up" meter was on high alert.

After a deep breath, he said, "We-really-would-like-to-have-Angel-with-us-for-Christmas." He spoke so quickly, it sounded like his sentence was just one word.

"What?" I shot up straight in the chair. Leaning over, I placed the iPad on the table, and that's when I caught a glimpse of Angel, standing by the door, shifting from one foot to the other.

I'd forgotten that my daughter was still in the room, clearly listening to every word.

"Please," Angel mouthed. "Please, Mom."

I shook my head at Angel, and to Bobby I said, "You must've forgotten. Angel spends Thanksgiving with you and Christmas with me."

"I know, I know," Bobby said. "But this is gonna be a special Christmas. Not only are Caroline's and my parents coming, but it's my parents' fiftieth anniversary, and we're having a special Christmas dinner for them."

Bobby paused, and I waited for him to tell me what all of his special plans had to do with our daughter. Bobby knew me well enough to already know that I would never give up Christmas with Angel.

When I remained silent, Bobby said, "So..."

I said, "So?"

"Awww, come on, Asia."

"No," I said.

"Yes!" Angel shouted.

I didn't even bother to cover up the phone when I yelled, "Go to your room!"

"Why? What did I do?" Angel whined.

"I need to talk to your father..."

"But I already know what you guys are talking about. Please, Mom! Please let me spend Christmas with Dad and Mom Caroline this year?"

I did my best not to cringe, but I cringed anyway. Angel had been calling Bobby's wife "Mom Caroline" ever since our custody agreement had been put in place when Angel was just five.

I hated that. Caroline wasn't a "mom" anything. She hadn't pushed and screamed a child through her birth canal. But I did my best never to complain about Caroline because, without her, Bobby might have full custody of Angel due to the stupid move I'd made when Bobby left me.

All I'd been trying to do was to get him back...make him pay for hurting me. I'd seen women do it on all the soap operas—so, I set Bobby up. I tried to have him arrested for molesting Angel.

But my lies, my trick, my plan was exposed, and Bobby was livid. When he told me he was going to take Angel from me, I went on my knees to his wife. I begged her, and she talked to Bobby. Hence, shared custody.

So even though I didn't like Caroline and she didn't like me, I tried to keep the haterade down—when it came to Angel.

"Mom, please. Just let me go this one time," Angel said bringing me back to the present. "Let me spend this Christmas with Dad and Mom Caroline, and I promise I'll spend every holiday with you for the rest of my life." Angel's hands were pressed together as if she were praying...or begging.

If Bobby weren't on the other end of the phone asking for something so ridiculous, I would've laughed at Angel. Always the drama queen. But I couldn't even chuckle 'cause there was not a damn thing funny.

"Seriously, Mom. I'll be ninety and you'll be two hundred and five, and we'll still be spending Christmas together. I promise."

I frowned. "Not funny. Now, I need to talk to your father by myself, so just step out, okay?"

With a final pout, Angel moonwalked out of the room. "Please," she said once again. "Remember until you're two hundred and five!"

"You're not helping your cause." I pointed my finger at Angel before I scooted from the chair and closed the door behind her. I knew my daughter; I was sure she would stay in the hallway and have her ear pressed to the door. But I didn't care what Angel heard, and in fact, she probably needed to hear some of the choice words I had for Bobby Johnson.

Going back to the phone, I said, "Bobby, I don't know what your game is..."

"Whoa! Game? What game? I'm just talking about spending Christmas with my daughter, and I already told you why."

"No," I shook my head so hard, a headache wouldn't be far behind. "Angel has always spent Christmas with me."

"And maybe that's one reason why she should spend one Christmas with me."

"That's not part of our custody agreement."

"I thought we were way past that, Asia. I thought I could just come to you. Didn't know I needed a court order for Christmas."

I pressed my lips together to hold the curses back. Then, I asked, "Is that a threat?" through clenched teeth. I didn't even give him a second to respond. "Are you saying that you'd go to court, get an order, and then leave me sitting at home by myself on the one holiday that I look forward to all year?" I huffed, "Oh, that's special, Bobby. Just treat me any ole kind of way. I'm just the mother of your daughter," then, just to be mean, I added, "the only child you have."

In the pause that followed, I could tell that I'd made my point. I didn't know why Caroline and Bobby never had children, but right now, Angel was his only child. And since that made the score one to zero—in my favor—I had the upper hand.

"Okay," Bobby said a bit softer. "I can see where you're coming from. And I'm not trying to take Angel away from you on Christmas."

"Good." That was all I had to say.

But right as I was about to push the "End" button on the screen, I heard Bobby say, "Why don't you come and spend Christmas with us, too?"

The victory I'd just felt made a U-Turn. "What?"

"Yeah, yeah," Bobby said as if he were warming up to his own idea. "Yeah, we really would like to have you and Angel come to

Christmas dinner...and your Aunt Beverly, too. We can make it a real family affair."

A pause, and then I busted out laughing. I mean, really laughing. Like throw my head back laughing. Like soon my stomach would be hurting laughing.

"What's so funny?"

"You! You got jokes."

"I'm not kidding," Bobby said.

"You have to be. Or have you had a divorce that you haven't told me about?"

"Oh, now you got jokes."

"It has to be a joke if you think Caroline, your wife who hates me, would spend her Christmas with me."

"First of all, she doesn't hate you."

"Ninja, please. The wife always hates the mistress." I wanted to add, especially if the mistress was more beautiful. But the thing was, Caroline and I looked a lot alike. "I can promise you that Caroline doesn't want me in your home."

"Oh, yeah? Hold on a second?"

I had no idea why Bobby put me on hold, and I tapped my freshly pedicured toes on the floor, wishing that I'd never taken the call. This was pure foolishness, and I didn't have time. Especially since this was the Saturday before Christmas, and although I'd finished my gift shopping for everyone else, this was when I loved to shop for myself. I loved being in that mix of confusion with all the last-minute shoppers. All of that pushing and shoving—that was the real spirit of Christmas.

With a sigh, I pulled the cell phone from my ear and looked at the minutes ticking away. Four minutes! Really? This call was already three minutes and forty-five seconds too long.

Then, "Hello."

I frowned but said nothing.

"Hello," came through the phone again.

"Uh..."

"Asia, this is Caroline."

"Oh...yeah." And then I grimaced. Caroline Fitzgerald Johnson always made me feel like a fool. She was one of those high-brow, well-bred women who didn't know a thing about the way I'd grown up. "What's up?" I asked, then I growled inside. What's up? Was that the best I could do?

"Well, Bobby just filled me in rather quickly," Caroline said in what I called that upper-class tone of voice. "And, I agree. We really want Angel here with us for Christmas, and," then there was a pause that lasted so long that I thought she'd hung up, "we'd love to have you, too."

Translation: We really want Angel, and I'll take you if that's the only way we can have her. Yeah, that's what Caroline meant. See, hoochie-game recognized hoochie-game. Now, I'm not saying I'm a hoochie, and I'll be nice and say that neither is Caroline. But we had both gotten Bobby in some kind of way. He was a star basketball player, and under those circumstances it was never an ordinary dating situation. Caroline and I had both done whatever we had to do to get that man. And that meant we both knew how the other operated.

So, I knew what she was thinking. And I knew there was no way the wife wanted to spend Christmas with the mistress. Especially since I wasn't any ole mistress; I was a ten-year-long mistress who'd given birth to her husband's child.

A few moments passed, but I still didn't say anything.

So Caroline spoke up, "I'm going to put Bobby back on the phone...and I really do hope you'll join us, Asia. And your Aunt Beverly, too."

"She'll be in New York for Christmas."

"Oh, that's too bad...maybe next year." And then Caroline was gone.

As I waited for Bobby to return, I paced. I had to figure this out—what was their game? What was their plan?

When Bobby called out my name, I asked, "What are you guys up to?"

"What?"

"When your wife wants to celebrate with your mistress, something's up."

"You're not my mistress..."

"Anymore." I said.

"Not for the last ten years."

"It's only been six years, Bobby."

"However long it's been, my point is that a lot of time has passed; we've been through a lot, but Caroline and Angel have their own relationship, and it's a really good one. And not only Caroline, but her parents, too. They love Angel just like my parents do. And none of them get to spend enough time with her. This Christmas is the perfect time for that."

His genuineness came straight through the phone. Maybe Bobby didn't have a plan. Maybe this was exactly what he said it was—just a way to bring Angel closer to his family.

But now I had a new problem—if Bobby drew Angel closer to his family, where would that leave me? "I don't know..."

"Okay, I respect that," Bobby said, surprising me. After he'd put Caroline on the phone, I'd been sure that he wouldn't take no for an answer. He said, "We still have a few days; just think about it."

"Why?"

"Why what?" he asked.

"I get why you want Angel there, but why me?"

"'Cause like you said, I don't want you to be alone when there's no reason for it. Plus, it really is time for us to put the past all the way in the past and build a new future."

I rolled my eyes. "When I think about my future, I don't think about spending time with you and your wife."

"Well, we're all a part of the same family—Angel's family. We all love her, and that's what's most important."

That sounded good, so why didn't it feel good, too?

He added, "And Angel wants to do this."

"Yeah, thanks a lot for that. Thanks for setting it up so it's going to be hard for me to say no to her."

"It's still going to be your decision, so just let me know."

Without saying goodbye, I pressed "End" and slumped back down into my pedicure chair. "Ugh," I growled. I couldn't believe this. There was no way to win this fight. Angel wanted it too much, and now that I was invited, there wasn't a real reason to say no.

Except for the fact that I didn't want to spend Christmas with my ex-lover and his wife and both of their parents. What kind of celebration would that be?

I could understand all of the grandparents wanting to spend time with Angel, but couldn't they do that at a wedding or a funeral, the way normal Americans got together?

I shook my head. I had no idea what I was going to do.

"Oh, holy..." and then, just before I muttered what I really wanted to say, I thought about the season and edited my words. Taking a deep breath, I said, "O' Holy...Night!"

Four

Sheridan

I slipped into the booth across from Kendall and Asia. "Sorry I'm late," I said to both of them.

"Do we look like we care?" Asia held up her martini glass as if she was about to give a toast, but then she took a sip instead. "Thank you for choosing the Martini Bar for our prayer meeting." She giggled.

"A prayer meeting?" I said with a frown. I was about to tell Asia not to say something so blasphemous. As if I would call a prayer meeting in a bar. But I didn't have to say a word. Kendall would handle Asia; she never let her get away with anything. It was like a torque reaction—Asia opened her mouth and Kendall threatened to punch her in it. So I just sat back and waited for the battle.

From the first day when Pastor Ford had asked me to lead a prayer group for women who, like me, were having challenges dealing with their exes, Kendall and Asia had gone at it. Each time, it was like watching prizefighters in a championship boxing match.

Yet, though they fought, they loved each other, too. It amazed me how close we'd all become. Our hangouts were just about a weekly thing, where we shared our trials, our tribulations, and brought all of our cares to each other. We talked, we laughed, we prayed.

And it wasn't just about the bad times, either. We were all at good points in our lives and often we got together to celebrate triumphs, too. Since 2007, meeting up with Kendall and Asia had been some of the highlights of my weeks.

And that was the reason why I'd called this get-together. Having been through their own ex-capades, as we liked to call it,

I knew they would understand and help me get through this train wreck of a Christmas I was sure to have with Quentin. I could just feel it coming...I felt it in my spirit. So I needed my girls, Kendall and Asia.

That was when I noticed it; Kendall hadn't said a word, and not only that, she was sitting there with a drink in front of her. Now call me crazy, but the brown liquid that filled that screwdriver glass didn't look a thing like the water that was always my fitness girlfriend's drink of choice.

"What's that?" I asked. I forgot all about the manners that my mother had taught me; I pointed my finger straight at Kendall's drink.

Kendall held my stare, then, with her eyes still on me, she lifted that glass and took a long, long swallow. The way she pursed her lips and squeezed her eyes shut, I guess the drink burned as it made its way down her throat. Finally, she said, "This is a whiskey sour."

"A whiskey sour? You?"

"Uh...yes...me," Kendall replied with the same force behind her words that I guess I'd just used. "Do you see anyone else here?"

"She could've thought your drink belonged to me," Asia said as she took another sip of her own martini. "You know I can handle two."

When Asia giggled again, I wanted to take that drink away from her, but my focus was on Kendall. Clearly something was wrong. First, Kendall never drank anything stronger than water...well, except sometimes she would go for it and have an unsweetened iced tea. But my friend was all about being healthy and not drinking her calories. "I'm just surprised," I said to Kendall. "That's all."

"Well, things change. Nothing stays the same." Kendall paused and swallowed hard as if she were fighting to hold back words or tears. "And anyway, if you didn't want me to drink, why did you set up this prayer meeting in the Martini Bar?"

This time, Asia laughed out loud. "See what I'm saying? This *is* a prayer meeting."

I shook my head. "No it's not. We're just girls getting together because, today, I needed a drink!" I glanced around, and when I saw one of the waiters looking our way, I raised my hand and waved at him.

Kendall and Asia's eyebrows rose in sync, but they didn't say a word until I gave my order to the waiter. "I'll have a pomegranate martini."

"Pomegranate?" Asia and Kendall said together.

More laughter from Asia before she took another sip leaving just a drop of liquid in her glass. "It's about to go down at this meeting," she said with so much cheer, I thought she was about to get up and dance. "Y'all are always calling me the lush—but not today. I think the two of you are gonna hold it down for me!" When Kendall and I stayed silent, Asia asked, "Okay, somebody better tell me something. What's wrong? I mean, aren't we all supposed to be merry with Christmas?"

"It's not Christmas until the day after tomorrow," Kendall snapped. "Don't rush it."

I agreed, "I'm not ready for any kind of Christmas."

Asia frowned. "Well, I know why I'm not filled with holiday cheer," she said, suddenly solemn, "but what's y'all's excuse? Last week, y'all were deep into the holidays."

"A lot can happen in a week," Kendall growled.

"Exactly," I said, "and that's the reason why I wanted to meet up—because I need help; I need you to talk me through something."

"Well, I'm glad you hit us up 'cause I need to talk, too," Asia said; all of her laughter was gone now.

I glanced at Kendall, but she lowered her eyes and stared at her glass.

"So," Asia began, "what's your drama? And before you answer, I bet it's not as bad as mine."

"I bet mine's worse," I said, answering Asia, though I kept my eyes on Kendall, as she kept her eyes on the bottom of her drink. I figured that if I just started talking, Kendall would come around. She always had an opinion, and as soon as I told her what was going on with me, she'd forget about what had her so down. So I said, "Are you ready for this? It seems like I'm going to have to spend Christmas with Quentin."

"Get out," Asia exclaimed. "That's what I wanted to talk about. I'm gonna be in my own Christmas prison...with Bobby and his wife." That thought made her slump lower in her chair. "You go first; I don't think I can talk about mine yet," Asia said as she raised her glass, indicating to the waiter that she wanted another martini.

My frown deepened. I couldn't believe that my news hadn't made Kendall sit straight up. Or at least look at me. But if it weren't for her eyelashes fluttering every few seconds when she blinked, I would've thought that Kendall was asleep.

But I started talking anyway. Before I finished, Kendall would be right there with me. "It's because of Christopher," I started. And then, I told how I was being emotionally blackmailed into having what I knew was going to be the worst Christmas.

"It doesn't sound so bad," Asia said when I finished.

"How can you say that? You know I don't really like Quentin after all he put me through," I said.

"That's my point," Asia said. "You're in a better place because not liking him is better than loving him." Asia sighed. "I still love Bobby. Yeah, I'll admit it," she said, as if I didn't know that.

Maybe Asia thought it was a secret, but the world knew that she still loved Bobby Johnson. Asia did a good job of pretending not to care. But it was clear every time Asia uttered Bobby's name that her heart belonged to him.

"Yeah, I still love him," Asia sniffed, as the waiter handed her another drink. "And now, I have to spend Christmas with the man I love and the woman he loves." She paused, and then wailed, "I don't want to do it!"

Oh, my god! I shrank down in my seat, then glanced around the bar hoping that no one was looking at us. It seemed, though, that the Christmas muzak that played through the speakers above was louder than Asia's cries.

But clearly, Asia was in some kind of distress.

"Well, if you don't want to do it, don't," I whispered, hoping that Asia would take my hint and lower her voice.

"I have to." Asia sobbed loudly. "If I want to spend Christmas with my precious little girl, then I have to do it with Bobby and Caroline, too." And then, Asia told her story. She repeated the phone call she'd had with Bobby word for word and ended with, "If I don't do it, I'll spend Christmas alone because Aunt Beverly is in New York until the day after Christmas." She paused and squinted as if she just had a new thought. "Actually, that's probably a good thing 'cause you know how my aunt gets down...always preaching. She'd probably pray over dinner that God blesses Bobby and Caroline so that they'll have a long, long marriage," she moaned. "She wouldn't say anything good about me and Bobby at all!"

Now I knew for sure that Asia'd had too much to drink. Did she really expect her aunt, our pastor, to say something positive about her affair with a married man? Pastor Ford had always outwardly disapproved of Asia and Bobby.

"Aunt Beverly just never understood," Asia cried, continuing what I felt was some kind of drunken rampage. "No one did. I love Bobby, and as the mother of his only child, we were supposed to be together...forever," she bawled.

As Asia cried, I shook my head and looked down at my drink. If my martini was going to have me acting like that, I needed to get something else. I was just about to lift my hand to call the waiter over and get a glass of water, when...

"You think you got problems."

Slowly, I brought my hand back down, and Asia and I turned to Kendall. She'd whispered her words, but we'd heard her clearly enough. We both sat there, silently, waiting for Kendall to say a little bit more.

A couple of beats and then, "I have to spend Christmas with my sister...and my ex-husband." Kendall still didn't look up.

"Oh, em, gee!" Asia exclaimed. "Are you freakin' kiddin' me? How did this happen? All three of us have to spend Christmas with our exes!"

"But mine will be worse than yours," Kendall said softly.

Asia sucked her teeth and took another sip. "Why is yours worse, Kendall? I just sat here and poured my heart out about how I love Bobby." She pounded her chest. "At least you don't love Anthony," Asia went on. "So mine is much worse than yours and Sheridan's combined."

Kendall still hadn't raised her eyes, but when she shook her head, tears slid down her checks and into her still half-filled glass.

I jumped up and rushed to the other side of the booth. I scooted onto the seat next to Kendall, pushing Asia against the wall. But I ignored her shouts as I wrapped my arms around Kendall. "Honey, what's wrong?" I lowered my head so that I could see Kendall's face; her skin was soaked with tears.

My goodness! Had Kendall been crying that much while we'd been sitting here? How had I missed it?

"Please, Kendall, tell me what's wrong."

Asia answered for her, "She just told you she has to spend Christmas with Sabrina and Anthony, and she thinks that's something to cry about. But I don't understand what's the big deal. She doesn't have to do it," Asia said as if Kendall wasn't sitting right there. "There aren't any children involved like with you and me. Kendall can just stay home. But my deal...I have to go," Asia sobbed before she took another gulp of her martini.

If I could've reached around Kendall, I would've slapped some sense into Asia. But instead, I did my best to ignore her, at least for the moment, and give all my attention to Kendall.

"Please, honey, tell me what's wrong?" When Kendall gave me nothing, I decided to try the Asia route. "Well, maybe you don't have to spend Christmas with them. I know you'd only do it because of your dad..."

As soon as I mentioned Kendall's father, Kendall's shoulders quaked, and now she sobbed out loud, too.

"So, why don't you spend Christmas with us?" I asked, trying to get the words out quickly. I was thinking that was a great solution. Kendall had joined me for Christmas a couple of times over the years. Most of the times, she celebrated the holiday out of town with friends—at least that's what she told me, though I can't say that I always believed her. I had a feeling that Kendall spent many of those Christmases alone. Something that she once told me she loved to do.

That's why I couldn't figure this out. Kendall said she would never be around Sabrina and Anthony again. Now when most people told me something that they would never do, I always said, "Never say never." It was a cliché, but the truth was, no one ever knew what they would do—except for Kendall, the exception to that cliché. When she said never, she meant it. And nothing would change her mind.

Except...something *had* changed. Something that had her so upset.

"Spend Christmas with us," I said. "And then you can spend the day after Christmas with your dad."

Kendall went from sobbing to wailing.

"I can't do that," Kendall cried. "I can't wait for the day after Christmas. I have to be there on Christmas."

I was trying to remember if I'd ever seen Kendall cry before. Even if I had, I knew it wasn't like this. I was sure that Kendall cried in private; didn't we all? But in public, she was the rock amongst us. She hardly showed any emotion—except for anger mixed with a pinch of bitterness.

But this...Kendall's sorrow was palpable. I asked her again, "Tell me what's going on. Why do you have to be there?"

"Because I have to," she sniffed. "Because...my dad...he's dying."

Those words stopped me cold. And even Asia, who had been sipping on another martini, had to put her glass down.

I asked, "What?"

Before Kendall could answer, Asia piped in with her own questions. "Dying? What's wrong with him? How does he know?" She didn't give Kendall a chance to respond before Asia added, "I don't think he's dying. I think he just said that to get you to finally have Christmas dinner with them."

Asia spoke with confidence, as if her words were the truth. But I knew her well enough to hear that little shaking right beneath her words. And I was pretty sure that Kendall could hear it, too.

"Kendall, are you sure?" I asked.

She nodded. "Yes." Her voice was a bit stronger now. "My dad is dying. He has breast cancer."

Together, Asia and I shrieked, and then Asia said, "That's impossible; men don't get breast cancer."

"Not that many, not that often, but my dad has always...done things a little differently," she wept.

This time, I didn't try to quiet my friend. All I did was hold her, rock her, and cry with her. And Asia cried, too, though her tears didn't stop her from raising her hand to call for the waiter.

From the corner of my eye, I saw the young man rushing to our booth. "Is everything all right here?" His eyes moved from Asia to me to Kendall.

We had to look like a hot mess, the three of us sitting on one side of the table, squished together, crying together. But I didn't care, I didn't move. I just kept my arms around Kendall and rocked.

The waiter asked, "Is there anything I can get you?" I didn't miss the way he glanced over his shoulder, looking like what he wanted to get was security.

"Yeah," Asia said with tears dripping down her face. "You can get us another round of everything."

Kendall and I hadn't even finished our first drinks, but I didn't bother to point that out. As the waiter rushed away, from the other side, Asia wrapped her arms around Kendall, too.

And with just two days left before Christmas, the three of us sat there and cried together.

Joy to My World

Sheridan Hart Goodman

Five

I stared at my reflection in the mirror, half expecting the image to speak back to me saying, "What in the world?"

But instead, I did the talking. "I can do this." And then I repeated those words over and over, praying that repetition would be good for my soul.

Days had gone by since I'd agreed to this, but still, I was feeling some kind of way. It was true that I'd shared some wonderful holidays with Quentin in the past, but I'd long ago forgotten what that was like, and I didn't want to be reminded.

I'd been happy with my non-relationship with Quentin. Of course, we had to speak occasionally because of the children. But now that both Christopher and Tori were grown, we hadn't had too many shared occasions in recent years. And whenever we did have to breathe the same air, with the exception of graduations, it had never been for more than fifteen minutes or so.

Today though, we'd have to share the same space; he'd be in my house for more than a few minutes, and that was the part that I couldn't get over.

I needed to change my focus, I needed to see this for what it was—just one simple day, one simple dinner; that's what I had to keep telling myself.

The problem was I couldn't get myself to believe that. There was nothing simple about Dr. Quentin Hart. Everything about him was always so extra. He couldn't live life the way normal people did—and the way he'd ended our marriage proved this.

Maybe what bothered me was that this wasn't just Christmas. This was the anniversary of our breakup. It was around this time of year, ten days after Christmas to be exact. New Year's 2004.

I moved away from the mirror, sat down on the bed, and remembered it all.

"Sheridan, I've fallen in love with someone else," Quentin had said to me the moment Christopher and Tori left for their first day back to school after the Christmas break.

At first, I'd just stood there, and then my eyes glanced at the TV on the kitchen counter because surely my devoted husband hadn't spoken those words.

But the words had come from Quentin, and my worst fear had come true: My gynecologist-husband had bonded and fallen in love with a patient during one of those intimate Pap smears!

When I realized what was happening, my first instinct was to kill Quentin, then hunt down this other woman and make her wish that she'd chosen another doctor.

But then, Quentin had clarified. "It's not another woman...I'm in love, but not with a woman. I'm in love with a man. I've fallen in love with Jett Jennings."

That was when the rumbling began. The rumbling that rose up through the soles of my feet and made its way up to my fists. I can't really explain what happened next, but it had something to do with my fist making a connection in a kick-boxing, upper-cut move that I'd just learned—and Quentin ended up on the floor.

I have no idea how long he was out. I didn't stay to help him. I just stepped right over him and went up to my bedroom.

Of course, I kicked him out of our house that night. Of course, it was all so painful for me. There were so many questions, especially the one regarding what my role was in all of this.

But you know what? I had not only survived; I'd thrived.

So now that I'd made it through all of that, now that I'd been delivered from Quentin, now that I had united with the man of any woman's dreams, Quentin was going to have a starring role in our own rendition of Guess Who's Coming to Dinner.

It was just too ridiculous to me.

But I had to find a way, so I started my mantra again. "I can do this," I kept whispering.

"Yes, you can."

I looked up, and there was my husband, leaning against the doorjamb, with his arms crossed and one leg in front of the other. He'd been there awhile, I could tell. And since he'd been staring at me, I decided to spend a few moments taking in the wonder of this man that I had the privilege to call my husband.

Looking at him now brought back some great memories. Like the first time I had the pleasure of laying my eyes on him. And I smiled as I thought about what had captured my attention. It was his uniform. Or rather, his body in his uniform. The UPS uniform that didn't make me have to use my imagination to see the roundness of his biceps or the tightness of his abs. I'd even taken a peek at his butt that day, even though I met him while he was walking down the aisle in the sanctuary delivering a package to the church.

I knew I needed to repent then—at the very least, throw myself across the altar. But thank God, I didn't have to repent now for the thoughts that were going through my head.

"What's wrong?" he asked, as he strode toward me.

"Absolutely nothing," I said, looking him up and down. "Positively nothing."

"Well, something's wrong," he said, taking my hand.

Clearly, he didn't know what I'd been thinking.

He said, "You've been sitting on this bed, just staring into space."

Seeing him had made me forget. But now, I remembered. Quentin!

"So, do you want to tell me what this anxiety is all about? Why don't you want Quentin here?"

"I don't know," I said, shaking my head. "I guess I don't like the idea of him walking in on our wonderful life; I don't want to share our holiday, our good times, with him."

"It's not like he's moving in, baby. He'll just be here for a couple of hours. Right after dinner, we can throw him out. We don't have to even let him stay for dessert."

He laughed, but I didn't because I was thinking that might be a good idea. I took an extra moment, really considering that proposition. Then, "That won't work," I said. "We're trying to make a good impression on Evon, remember?"

"Darn," Brock joked. "But seriously, I hope this isn't about any concerns you have about me. I like the fact that Quentin will be here."

That's what Brock had been saying ever since Christopher asked me to do this. "Why?" I asked him. "Why do you like it so much? Why did you agree to this?"

"Because you two share children, and one day, you'll share grandchildren. He has to be a part of our tradition."

I did it gently, but I pulled my hands away from him and crossed my arms. "I don't like it."

He chuckled a bit as the tips of his fingers grazed my bare arms, and I knew he'd done that on purpose. He knew that he made me shiver and quiver every time he touched me.

Brock knelt down in front of me and made me unfold my arms. "It's gonna be all right. I promise," he said.

"I remember a time when you didn't like Quentin."

"That's not true. I've never disliked him. I just wanted to make sure that he no longer had your heart." He paused. "Once you gave your heart to me, I've been cool with him ever since."

I twisted my lips. "I don't know if I'd be so gracious with any of your exes."

"There's a difference between an ex-spouse and an ex-girlfriend. This is about family, and we're always gonna be about that."

How could I be mad at that? I cupped the side of his face with the palm of my hand. "When I grow up, I wanna be like you."

We laughed together because that was our little joke. I had some years on Brock—almost nine. But while I had those years over him chronologically, he had decades over me emotionally.

The doorbell interrupted our little time together. Pushing himself up, he reached for my hand. "Come on," he said. "Let's go greet our guests. Let's embrace our new traditions."

When I stood, I sighed and hugged him. Then I wrapped my arm around his waist and together, we walked out of our bedroom.

Six

"I'll get it!" Tori bellowed before she blew through the upstairs hallway and down the stairs. Brock and I had to jump back to avoid the aftermath of what felt like a hurricane as she ripped by us, right as we stepped from our bedroom.

I watched my daughter and laughed. Being nineteen and a junior in college didn't stop Tori from acting like she was still thirteen. She was still the first one to answer a ringing telephone or a knock at the door.

"Christopher!" Tori yelped the moment she opened the door. She jumped into his arms.

The two shopping bags he held dropped from his hands as he gripped the doorway to balance himself against the force of his sister. "Yo, squirt. Give me a moment to get inside, will ya?"

"I can't help it," she said. "I've missed my big brother!" Then she planted rapid-fire kisses on his neck and cheek, making all of us laugh. It was a kiss attack. But after too many seconds of making him hold her up, Tori jumped down and turned to Evon. "Hey, girl," she said, giving her future sister-in-law a hug.

"Welcome home," Evon said, even though she was still laughing. "You got in last night?"

"Yeah, and I can't believe my brother didn't come over to see me."

"You got home after eleven!" Christopher protested.

"So? What did you have to do that was better than seeing your baby sister?"

I didn't miss the exchange between Christopher and Evon. The way he glanced at her, and with a grin, she lowered her eyes.

"Uh...I was sleeping," Christopher said to Tori. "You expected me to get out of bed?"

"Yes I did, but whatever. You'll have plenty of time to make that up to me."

"I know, I know. You're home for a month, right?"

"You know what?" Tori said. "I don't want to talk about school, and I don't want to hear about work. She spread her arms wide in the air. "It's Christmas!"

"She's right." I hugged Christopher, then turned to Evon. "Merry Christmas, sweetheart," I said as I pulled her into my arms. She felt like my daughter-in-law already.

"Merry Christmas, Mrs. Goodman," she said, and then she gave me that smile that could earn her a fortune in a toothpaste commercial. "Thank you for having me." Holding out a foil-covered cake plate, she added, "I baked a little something. I hope you don't mind?"

Mind? Was she kidding? This girl had everything, and she baked, too?

"You didn't have to do that," I said, but I hugged her again before I took the plate from her.

Before I had a chance to tell Evon how delighted I was to have her *and* the cake with us, Christopher stepped back and held up the shopping bags that Tori had knocked from his hands just moments before. "We come bearing gifts."

"Good, big bro," Tori said, grabbing one of the bags from him. "'Cause now that you're making the big bucks over at Disney, you know I'm expecting the biggest and baddest gift ever."

"Oh, don't worry. You're gonna love what I got you." He tapped his fist softly on her head. "Now, the big question is, what did you get me?"

"Haven't you heard? I'm a starving college student!" Tori exclaimed. "I have no money, and I won't for about the next two decades. Because after I graduate and then go to law school, I'll have to work the next ten years to pay off student loans."

"Yeah, right." Christopher laughed and waved his finger in her face. "I'm not falling for that. We have the same parents. Mom and Dad have been saving for your college education since the beginning of time."

All I could do was smile as I turned away from my children and took Evon's cake into the dining room. I sat the plate right in between the sweet potato pie and lemon pound cake.

I'd only been gone a couple of minutes, but when I returned to the living room, my children were in full sibling banter, with Evon and Brock on the sidelines, laughing. I stood at the edge of the living room, taking mental pictures. If I could just keep moments like this in my heart and my mind forever, my life would be completely fulfilled.

"What's all that noise?"

I turned toward the staircase and there was my mother, Beatrice, slowly descending. She held a cane in one hand but wasn't using it, instead leaning her weight on the banister.

In five seconds flat, Brock jumped up from the sofa and dashed into the foyer, where he took the steps two at a time until he reached her. Then he held out his arm, and she grabbed ahold of him as he led her down the rest of the way.

I was about to make my way over to give my mother her morning kiss, but I was knocked out of the way by her grandchildren.

"Merry Christmas," rang through the air over and over again. Hugs and kisses came after that, and then too many arms tried to lead my mom into the living room. But she swatted every single one of them away.

"I can do this by myself!" my seventy-three year old mother grumbled, but with a smile on her face.

They all backed off and held up their hands as if surrendering, and then we all watched my mom balance on her cane and walk slowly into the living room.

I held my breath as I always did when my mom maneuvered with only the assistance of the cane. Not that she had ever fallen or given me cause for concern in this way. It was just that I was watching my mother get older, and she had especially aged after my dad passed away. It had been so tough losing Dad, but it was tougher seeing my mother without my father at her side.

That's why from the moment Dad died in 2005, I'd wanted to scoop my mom up and move her in with me. But Beatrice Collins wasn't giving up any part of her freedom, and she fought me like we were in a world war to maintain her independence. She'd wanted to stay in that home where my brother and I had been raised.

Every few weeks, I talked to her about it, and she always told me no. Then, a few months ago, Brock asked me if he could give it a try. I told him to go for it, though I knew what her answer would be.

I stood and listened as he told my mother, "Let me explain what this means to me, Mom," he'd said. "My family needs you. We need to share as much time as possible with you. We need you for your wisdom; we need you to teach us how to really love. We need you to fill our home with your joy. If my mother were alive, we'd have her with us, too. But I feel just as blessed to have you. So will you do it? Will you move in with us?"

I'd expected her to say, "No, I'm good. " But instead, my mother had hugged him and said, "Okay, I will."

I couldn't believe it, but I wasn't gonna be mad that she'd listened to Brock and not me. A few weeks after that talk, my mom said goodbye to the home where she'd lived for almost fifty years, and she moved in with us to begin new traditions.

As Brock helped my mother get settled onto the sofa, I watched and marveled at just how gentle he was with her. I couldn't count the ways I loved this man.

Once my mother was comfortable in her place, the sounds of Christmas continued. There was no need for Christmas carols. My children teasing each other, my mother's chatter, and all of their laughter was all the music I needed.

I couldn't do anything but smile as I leaned against the wall and watched Christopher and Evon unpack the dozens of gifts, then pass them to Tori as she organized them under the tree.

I sighed.

"That's what I'm talking 'bout," Brock said as he wrapped his arms around me from behind.

"What?" I jumped, just a little. I hadn't even noticed my husband coming up to me.

"I love hearing that—that contentment from you and all of this noise from our children."

"That's not noise!" I laughed. "Don't you recognize Christmas when you hear it?"

He held me, and we just stayed there, standing, watching, and soaking up the joy.

Brock whispered, "We're beginning some new traditions today. First, there was just Christopher and Tori."

"And now we have Mom and Evon."

"Soon, Christopher and Evon will have children..."

I slapped his hand. "Hush your mouth. I'm not ready to be a grandmother."

"Who said anything about a grandmother? You're more like a glam-mother."

Okay, I had to laugh at that one. "I'll take that. But let's not forget Tori. She'll be getting married soon."

"Not that soon," Brock said. "She still has undergrad and then law school. And knowing our daughter, she'll want to rise to Attorney General before she thinks about any relationship."

Even though I didn't like it, I had to agree with Brock on this one. Whenever I asked Tori about guys, she changed the subject or told me that school and then her career were her priorities.

"There are too many unfortunate people who need my help, Mom. I can't think about a relationship right now."

In a way, I hated that. Not that I didn't think education was important, but I knew that the best success was when you had someone to share it with. I wanted my children to experience all the joy I had with Brock. But no matter what Tori decided to do, I was so proud of both of my children. They'd been through quite a bit when Quentin had left us, and thank God neither one suffered scars from the past.

Brock kissed the back of my head, then stepped away, and I released another sigh of contentment. This Christmas scene that played out in front of me was what life was all about.

Family. Love. Tradition.

Then the doorbell rang.

Just out of habit, I waited for Tori to make a move, but it didn't even seem like she heard the bell since she stayed at her spot near the tree. Chuckling, I turned toward the door.

Now, maybe it was because I'd been so caught up in Christmas that I forgot to think, I forgot to brace myself.

I opened the door...and then, I forgot to breathe.

There stood Quentin.

It had been a moment, at least a year since I'd seen Quentin, and my first thought was why hadn't he aged the way all humans were supposed to? And my next thought: What an absolute waste of fineness—sharing all of that with another man.

"Merry Christmas, Sheridan." Quentin stepped inside and kissed my cheek before I had a chance to respond.

I was just about to return his Christmas greeting, but he turned his body slightly. "I hope you don't mind; I bought a guest." He took a single step to the side so that I could see. "Sheridan, this is my fiancée."

I don't know what opened wider—my eyes or my mouth.

Quentin had to be kidding. No way would he do this. Not today. Not at Christmas!

Seven

Quentin stepped over the threshold and pulled the woman into the foyer with him. Her long ponytail swished from side to side as she bounced in like a cheerleader and greeted me with a smile that had probably cost thousands. The tautness of her face, the smoothness of her complexion, and the brightness of her eyes made me wonder how long had this girl been out of high school?

"Sheridan, this is Harmony McCray. Harmony, this is Christopher and Tori's mom, Sheridan Hart."

"So nice to meet you, Sheridan," she said in a voice that sounded like she was going to break out in a soprano solo at any moment.

There were so many things that I could've said, but the only thing that was on my mind was—Harmony was a woman! A very young woman!

She was dressed appropriately enough for Christmas in Los Angeles in what I thought was a silk, knee-length, green wrap dress. I guess you could say that the dress was classy. It would've been flattering on anyone, but the dress on Harmony looked like it was in a battle with her perky, over-grown boobs...and her boobs were winning.

But those weren't her only curves. I took inventory the way we women often do to other women. And from her calves to the swerve of her hips, the swoop of neck and what looked to be a completely flat stomach that had not been attacked by the kind of fat that seemed to love me, Harmony could've easily been in the running to be a *Sports Illustrated* swimsuit model—if the magazine ever decided to feature a woman who wore something larger than a size two. She would've been the perfect woman to introduce the world to a full-figured bikini-clad woman with a serious body.

"Actually, my wife's last name is Goodman." It was like he came out of nowhere when Brock stepped to my side. I guess he spoke for me since I was kinda frozen—in shock *and* silence.

"Oh, my bad," Quentin said as he shook hands with Brock. "Just habit, you know. Merry Christmas." And then Quentin did it all over again. With the same introduction that he'd just given to me, Quentin told Brock that he was engaged...to this woman.

I stood back and waited to see what Brock would do. But when all he said was, "Nice to meet you, Harmony. And Merry Christmas," I wondered if my husband had gone mad.

But then I heard the footsteps of the children, rushing from the living room. Brock may have missed it, but Christopher and Tori would have the same clarity that I had. They would see that none of this made any sense and my outspoken son would be the first to call out his father the way he always did.

I turned. I watched. I waited.

"Hey, Dad! Merry Christmas," Christopher and Tori spoke almost in sync.

And then...

They both turned toward the woman and greeted her.

"Merry Christmas, Harmony," Tori said with glee.

Christopher gave the woman his own Christmas greeting and then added, "Dad didn't tell us you were coming."

"Well, my plans changed," she said, looking up at Quentin in a way that I could only describe as lovingly. "I decided to stay in L.A. for the holidays."

"Well, I'm glad you came," Christopher said before he kissed the woman's cheek.

What? My children were acting as if they'd met this woman before. And not only as if they'd met her, but as if they knew her.

Well, maybe that wasn't such a big deal. Christopher and Tori did see their father and often didn't tell me. But even though they'd met this woman (Tori had probably hung out with her at a club or two), they clearly didn't know the most important thing.

"Uh...Christopher, Tori, this is Harmony," I said, taking a step toward them.

The two exchanged glances. "Yeah, Ma, we know," Christopher answered for both of them.

Okay...here comes the big blow. "Harmony and your father are...engaged." Then I took a step back because I didn't want to be in the line of fire.

Christopher and Tori looked at me with questions in their eyes and frowns on their face. The way they looked at me, I half expected one of them to ask, "Engaged in what?"

But instead, this time it was Tori who responded for both of them. "Yeah, Mom, we know." Then, as if it were no concern, Tori said to the woman, "Harmony, come and meet my grandmother."

Harmony followed Tori into the living room like she was already a part of the family. And Quentin rushed right behind his daughter...and his fiancée.

"My favorite mother-in-law," Quentin exclaimed before he opened up his arms, leaned over, and embraced my mother.

"Your only mother-in-law," my mom responded with a smile that made me want to growl.

"Not for long, Grandma," Tori said. "Dad's getting married again. And this is his fiancée, Harmony."

"Oh, really?" The smile that was on my mother's face made me want to stomp my foot and scream. Was I the only one who noticed the big fat elephant in the room? I wanted to remind them all that Quentin couldn't marry a woman. He'd tried that with me, and look at how that had turned out.

But the Christmas cheer went on, and as I stood on the sidelines and watched, Quentin and Harmony mixed in as if it were no big deal that a gay man had just introduced a woman as his fiancée.

"Sweetheart!"

It took a couple of blinks for me to turn to the sound of Brock's voice.

"You okay?"

I watched Quentin and Harmony for another moment before I said, "Can I speak to you...in the kitchen?"

He glanced over his shoulder and nodded. "Doesn't look like anyone will miss us."

I rushed ahead of him, moving to the place where the aroma of the slow-baking turkey welcomed us. Waiting for a moment, I stood in silence, making sure we hadn't been followed.

Then, "Did you see that woman, and did you hear what Quentin said?" I was trying to whisper, but it sounded more like a hiss.

"Do you see all of this food?" Brock answered as he lifted a corner of the foil that covered one of the seven dishes that lined the counter. "Man, I can't wait to get stuffed with your mom's stuffing."

"Brock!"

"What?"

"You're not listening to me."

"I am, but I know what you're talking about, and I don't want to talk about it."

"Quentin said he's getting married!" I exclaimed, not caring about what my husband had just said.

He leaned against the counter and sighed, as if he were giving into a conversation that he didn't want to have. Nodding, he said, "I guess you think it's weird that he showed up with her today."

"Uh...yeah."

"Well," Brock began to explain, "he probably only did it because it's Christmas, and he wanted Harmony to spend the afternoon with his children."

"If that were the only weird thing about this, I could handle it, but everything is out of order here. I mean, how old do you think she is?"

He frowned and shrugged. "I don't know. I don't care."

"What about the fact that he called her his fiancée? That means he's engaged." I stopped, and when Brock said nothing, I gave my husband further clarification. "Engaged...to be married."

"Uh...yeah."

"To a woman!"

He looked at me for a moment longer before he turned away and lowered his head to peek into another dish. "Babe, your macaroni and cheese looks so good."

"Brock! Doesn't Quentin saying he's getting married bother you?"

Once again, he faced me. "No," he shook his head, "and I'll only have a problem if it bothers *you*. Because I'll wonder why you're upset about it."

"I'm not upset...at least not in that way. I'm just trying to figure it out because Quentin's gay!"

Brock shrugged. "That's not my problem."

"Well, suppose Harmony doesn't know?"

"That's not your problem."

"I'm not saying it is. I'm just saying..."

Before I could say anything more, Brock held up his hand. "What Quentin does with his life has nothing to do with you. You don't need to be thinking or worrying about him."

His words were so true. I took a deep breath. "You're right. This is not my business. It's just that I'm..."

"Shocked," Brock finished for me. "I could tell because when Quentin introduced you as Sheridan Hart you didn't go off like you had when he did that before."

"Did he call me Sheridan Hart?" I was so surprised that it sounded like my voice went up an octave.

"See?" Brock laughed. "Yes, he did. But trust me, I understand your being surprised. But that part over there," he motioned with his head toward the living room, "that's his life. This part over here," he wrapped his arms around me, "is yours. And the only time these two lives will meet is at Christmas because of the children. And Christopher's wedding, of course. But besides that..." He stopped as if those three words were a complete thought.

I nodded.

"So, you okay?" he asked.

"I'm okay."

"And you can go back out there and handle this?"

I nodded, but only because I wasn't going to lie out loud. None of this felt normal enough to handle, but I was going to do what my husband wanted. I was going to return to the family festivities and pretend that life was exactly the way it was supposed to be, when Brock and everyone else in that living room knew that it wasn't.

But if they wanted to pretend, so would I. Today was going to be nothing less than one big fairy tale of a Christmas.

Eight

Maybe if I'd had time to talk to Tori while we were setting the table...but I didn't because Evon was there, helping. Or maybe if I'd had time to talk to my mother when we were setting out the food on the buffet...but I didn't because Evon *and* Harmony were there, helping. Maybe if I'd had time to talk to anyone before we all sat down to our Christmas lunch, I could've stopped the question that had been brewing inside of me.

At least I'd waited until after Brock blessed the food. He was carving the turkey while the rice and gravy, mac and cheese, collard greens, and yams made their way around the table.

The chatter continued as everyone talked about how good the food looked and gave their compliments to my mom, who'd prepared most of the dishes.

My mother had just given her thanks to everyone when my question slipped out of my mouth.

"So, Harmony, did you know that Quentin is gay?"

The world in that dining room stopped cold. Not another word was spoken, not another fork moved, even the air stopped circulating.

In the first moments, I wondered why the room had become so silent. It wasn't until I heard the groan from Christopher and saw the "oh-no-she-didn't" look from Tori that I realized I'd actually asked that question out loud.

I did a quick scan of the faces around the table and every single one of them was shocked. But I wanted to tell them all to stop looking at me that way. They all knew they wanted to ask the same thing.

But since the stares continued, I explained, "I mean...you know...Quentin and I were married for a long time...and I just wondered if he told you our story...since you're engaged...and all."

"Sheridan," my mother tapped her cane on the floor. "Can I speak to you in the kitchen?"

"Sure," I said, though I wondered what my mother could want right at this moment. Harmony was getting ready to give us the scoop, and I didn't want to get up and leave.

For a moment, I thought about asking my mother to wait, but here's the thing—even though I was grown, Beatrice Collins was a black mother. And with a black mother, there were just certain things you didn't do. Telling my mother to wait a few minutes was one of those things.

Everyone was still sitting there with their wide eyes on me. I just smiled and said, "I'll be right back," as if they would miss me. Then I followed my mom into the kitchen.

"What's up, Mom?"

My mother stared at me for so long that I started to get uncomfortable. "What's up?" she finally said. "I swear I raised you better!"

I squinted, trying to figure out what my mother meant. "What're you talking about?"

"How rude can you be?"

"What?"

"Asking Harmony that question."

My mother lost me there. "What was wrong with that? I just wanted to know if she knew."

"It was rude."

"No, it wasn't," I insisted. "I wish someone had asked me that before I married Quentin."

My mom sighed. "Is that what this is about? You're still mad at Quentin? After all of these years? After this wonderful life that you have?"

"I'm not mad at him, Mom. I just wanted to know how a gay man could suddenly be marrying a woman?"

"Why do you care?"

I shrugged. I wasn't sure if it was so much that I cared; I think it was more that I was curious. I think.

My mother said, "What he does and why he's doing it is none of your business. That's between Quentin and Harmony. It has nothing to do with you, it has nothing to do with your children, so you need to keep your nose out of it."

"I'm not..."

My mother went into that mom thing and held up her hand. "I'm not playing, Sheridan," she said. "We need to just go back in there and enjoy ourselves over all of that good food I slaved so hard to prepare. Just let everyone enjoy their Christmas, and you keep your curiosity to yourself."

What I wanted to do was cross my arms and stomp my feet since my mother

was treating me like an insolent teenager. But instead I nodded, then made a motion with my hand for my mother to go back to the dining room in front of me. Then I followed her.

Inside the dining room, the conversation continued as if no one had been disturbed by me or my question. And I have to say, that bothered me even more. I didn't care what my mother said; my mom and everybody else wanted to ask the same question. It was a perfectly normal question, and after what I'd been through with Quentin, I deserved an answer. After all, it wasn't like I'd gone to his home and gotten in his business. He'd brought this to my house.

But the fact that Harmony hadn't answered, and the fact that she seemed only to be surprised by how direct I was, made me believe that Harmony did know Quentin's history.

So, why was she with Quentin? What kind of woman would marry a gay man?

And then it hit me!

"So, Harmony, where are you from?" my mother asked.

At first, my mother's question threw me off. Wasn't she the one who had just told me not to ask questions? But then, I realized my mother and her questions were exactly what I needed to find out the truth.

So as Harmony talked, I listened and kept my eyes on her.

"From Detroit," Harmony said. She paused for a moment as she chewed the rest of the yams that she'd just put in her mouth. Then, "I was born and raised there. Stayed until I left for college."

I almost stopped her there to ask when she'd graduated from college since I was curious about her age, too. But I decided I'd keep my focus on one thing at a time.

Harmony kept talking about how she loved Detroit and hated what was going on in that city now. And as she talked, I kept my mouth shut and my eyes on her. I stared, I searched, I squinted, and then finally, I sighed.

Harmony's throat was as smooth as the rest of her skin; she didn't have an Adam's apple.

Harmony was born a woman. So there went that theory.

"How did you two meet?" my mother asked.

For someone who'd just told me to stop with the questions, my mother sure did have a lot of her own.

"We met at a nurses' convention where Quentin was speaking."

"Oh, you're a nurse?" I asked.

The room went silent, and it almost felt like everyone was holding their breath...as if they were waiting for me to add an addendum to my question. Something that would shock and embarrass them all.

But when I said nothing else, a huge exhale filled the room and Harmony answered.

"Yes; I'm an RN."

"In fact, that's how I actually met Harmony," Quentin piped in. "As she said, I was one of the presenters at their awards ceremony, and I presented her with her pin for fifteen years of service."

"Fifteen years?" my mother said before I could get the words out. "Really?"

Harmony laughed. "I know what you're thinking. Everyone says that I look so young. Sometimes when I walk into a patient's room, they ask to see my drivers' license."

"Well, you know what they say," Tori piped in. "Black don't crack." She waved her fork in the air.

"What you know about that?" When my mother asked that, everyone laughed...except for me.

I didn't see anything funny. Okay, so Harmony wasn't twenty-one like I originally thought. And though I thought she was still a little young for Quentin, who was I to judge when my younger husband was sitting right next to me. But age was only a number and not the issue. The issue was—Harmony was a woman.

"Well, black sure 'nuff don't crack," Quentin said. "I was up on that stage and when Harmony walked out, I was like, 'Bam!'"

Again laughter, again not from me. I tried to imagine that scene. Quentin on stage speaking, and then this voluptuous woman comes out...and then, what? Her looks made him stop?

No! I didn't believe that. Quentin wasn't into women.

That's why I couldn't help it. That's why another question slipped right through my lips. "So, Quentin, when did you stop being gay?" When the table quieted and Quentin frowned at me like he wanted to fight me, I explained, "I mean, what made you change your mind? I didn't know that could happen." I was hoping that at least somebody would look at me and nod their agreement. But just like before, no one looked like they were on my side.

"Oh, come on now." First, I looked at Brock, then, Tori, Christopher and Evon, and finally, my mother. "Y'all know you want to know. I'm just the only one bold enough to ask." No one said a word. So to lighten it up a bit, I added, "It kinda makes you want to say, 'Where they do that at?'" Again laughter, but this time, *I* was the only one who laughed.

Tori moaned, Brock shook his head, and my mother gave me a wicked side-eye glare.

Christopher said, "Ma, can I speak to you...in the kitchen?" He was already standing.

What did he want? I was tempted to tell him no, but then, when I glanced around the table, I thought it might be best for me to excuse myself, even if it were just for a moment.

I followed my son, and once we were alone, I faced him. Christopher stood, all six-feet-two of him looming over me. With his arms crossed and his lips pressed together, he presented quite a threatening picture.

Except for one thing—I was still the mama. And just like Beatrice Collins, I was a black mama, and Christopher knew that. So he wasn't going to take this too far.

That's why I said, "You have a problem with me asking questions, too?"

He nodded. "Yeah, your questions and your language."

I frowned. "Language?"

He freed his arms and held out his hands to me. "'Where they do that at?' Really, Ma?"

I laughed, but when Christopher didn't laugh with me, I said, "Oh come on. You know that was funny. I was just trying to take the edge off since everyone seemed so upset."

"You think?"

"What's the big deal, Christopher? You know everybody sitting at that table is thinking the same thing, but I'm the only one who has the guts to ask."

"No, Ma, that's not it. You're the only one thinking it, 'cause the rest of us are just gonna let Dad live his life. I mean, really, why do you care?"

Now, I had to pause. Because that was the same question that Mom had asked me. "I don't care," I said. "I'm just asking a few questions."

"Questions that are none of your business. Just leave it alone."

"It's just..."

"Come on, Ma, please. I invited Evon to have dinner with us because I knew you and Grandma were going to stick your foot in the food and she was gonna see all the love in our family."

"So how am I stopping that?"

"Because you're sticking your foot in your mouth. You're making everyone uncomfortable. Just stop it with all the questions!"

Why was everyone pretending that I was doing something wrong? I was just asking questions, and I wasn't going to stop until somebody gave me answers. But I looked into Christopher's eyes...and he was begging me.

"Okay," I said with a sigh. "I'll bite my tongue."

"And bite anything else you have to, please, Ma!"

"I said okay." And I would keep that promise. I would just do whatever I had to do to make it through the rest of this lunch. Maybe if I got Quentin and his fiancée out of here, my questions would go with him.

Yeah, that's what I would do. Just get everyone to finish up the rest of their lunch, gulp down their dessert, and twenty minutes from now, I'd be free!

With that plan in my mind, I hugged Christopher. "I'm sorry."

"It's all good. I just wanna make sure that Evon doesn't give me back that ring."

I was glad when Christopher chuckled with me. "She's not gonna do that. She knows she has a good thing in you."

"Yeah, but she might run for the hills after spending this afternoon with my crazy mama."

"Okay, okay. I get it." I followed Christopher back into the dining room where Evon stood, clearing away the dinner plates.

"I'll do that," I said, taking over. "You just sit down and enjoy yourself."

Ordinarily, I would've been happy for the help. And cleaning up with Evon, would've given me even more time to bond with her. But right now, I couldn't think about bonding. Every bit of energy had to go to keeping my mouth shut.

So cleaning up was a good distraction. Because busy hands keep the tongue silent. I was sure that was a scripture somewhere in the Bible. And if it weren't, it needed to be.

"Are you sure you don't want any help?" Harmony asked. "I'd be happy to." She pushed back her chair.

The sincerity in her eyes and her voice made me want to apologize for everything that I'd said. My intent was never to make anyone uncomfortable.

Before Harmony could rise all the way, though, I held up my hand. "No seriously. I just want everyone to have a good time today, so just stay here. I've got it under control." I paused and added, "But thank you," hoping that Harmony would understand that I meant no harm.

When Harmony smiled back, I was relieved. All was well, and the conversation once again resumed at the table.

While everyone chatted, I cleared the table. But even as I worked, the questions wouldn't leave me alone. And now, there was a new question tossed into the mix—why did I care?

Inside the kitchen, I took my time stacking the dishes on the counter. I was about to rinse them and then put them in the dishwasher, but instead, I just paced the length of the kitchen. All of these questions rolled around in my head. They wouldn't leave me alone, and I was afraid to go back into the dining room. Because something evil was going on in there. Something had control of my tongue, and I couldn't stop my thoughts from slipping out. If I had my way, I would've just stay in the kitchen. I wouldn't leave until everyone was out of the house.

But if I didn't get back out there soon, Brock would come looking for me and drag me back to the table to finish living our traditions.

So, I took a couple of deep breaths, said a couple of quick prayers, and just hoped that my tongue didn't operate without my brain. I fixed a smile on my face and strutted back into the dining room in time to hear Quentin say, "Son, you got yourself a good woman there."

Evon, who was setting out the dessert plates, smiled at Quentin; Christopher stood up and wrapped his arms around her. "Trust me, Dad, I know how blessed I am, and I can't wait to make her my wife. June can't get here fast enough."

"Oh really, June?" Harmony said. She glanced at Quentin with a grin. "You didn't tell me that, baby." And then to everyone else, she announced. "Quentin and I are thinking about a June wedding, too."

Oh, lawd! I groaned inside. If they wanted me to be quiet, this subject needed to be changed. So, I said, "We have sweet potato pie, a lemon cake made by my mom, and this beautiful coconut cake made by this lovely lady." I looked over at Evon. "So, tell me what you want, and I'll fill your plates."

It worked...at least for a few minutes. The focus was on everything sweet until every plate was filled with a slice of cake or a piece of pie.

And then, Harmony opened her mouth. "Evon, we really should coordinate about June." Then, looking at Evon and Christopher, she asked, "Do you have a date yet?"

Christopher held Evon's hand. "The first Saturday in June. But, I would marry her tomorrow if Mom weren't insisting on a big wedding."

Evon laughed. "It's both of our moms. They won't let us get away with eloping."

"You got that right," I said. And then I shut my mouth.

Then, Evon said, "I didn't know you guys were getting married already."

"Oh, yeah," Quentin chuckled, "when you get to be my age, you know what you know. No need to waste time."

Harmony laughed. "And at my age, if I want to have children, we need to get started."

I don't know what happened; my fork crashed to my plate and all eyes turned straight to me. "I'm sorry," I said. "But I just can't take it." I looked at Harmony. "Seriously? You want to have children with him? He's *gay*." To Quentin, I said, "Tell her!"

Quentin's eyes narrowed, and he kept his glare on me. But he spoke to my husband when he said, "Brock, would you mind if I spoke to your wife...alone?"

My eyes shot straight to Brock, and when he nodded and said, "If it's okay with her," I wanted to punch him in his eye. Really? He was just gonna let Quentin run things in our house? The way I was thinking, if Quentin had something to say, he needed to say it to all of us since he owed everyone an explanation. But once again, it was the expressions around the table that made me get up and stomp toward the kitchen. I could feel the heat of Quentin's anger following me.

Inside the kitchen, I crossed my arms and Quentin did the same. We stared each other down as if it were a contest, and finally, I broke the silence.

"What do you want?"

"Well, thank you for inviting me to your home and making me feel so welcomed."

I was about to tell him that I hadn't invited him, that he'd been forced on me. But I kept silent and waited for him to say more.

Finally, he threw up his hands and blew out a long breath. "What is your problem with me, Sheridan?"

"I don't have a problem; I have questions—there's a difference."

"Why do you have questions about my life?"

"Because I just want to know."

"Why, Sheridan? Why do you want to know?"

"Because...because...you were married to me for seventeen years, and then you left me."

He blinked as if he were confused. "I thought we were way past that. Especially once you married Brock."

"And now *you're* getting married."

"So? You've remarried; why do you care about me doing the exact same thing? Why do you care about me at all?"

Maybe it was because everyone had asked me the same question, maybe that was the reason why the answer finally burst right out of me.

"Because you didn't just leave me! You left me...for a man. You left your wife of seventeen years to join the other team. You changed your mind. And now, you're with a woman?"

He nodded slightly but said nothing.

I said, "So, what does that mean? That you're no longer gay? That you were only gay when you were with me? That I turned you gay?"

"Turned me gay?" he said, as if he had to repeat those words to get them right. "Why...why do you think what happened to me has anything to do with you?"

"Because when we got married, you were straight. Then, you became gay, and now, you're straight again. And the only time in there when you were gay is when you were with me."

"That's not true."

"It's not? So you're saying you're still gay, but you're going to marry Harmony anyway?"

He shook his head, then waited a moment as if he were thinking. Then, "Do you remember there was a time when I wanted us to get back together?"

I didn't acknowledge his words, but I did remember. It was months after I'd met Brock, right when Brock and I started getting serious. Quentin had made all kinds of overtures to me, tugging at my heartstrings, making me believe that I still had love for him.

It had been so confusing at the time. Seriously, I didn't know if I should look back or move forward. I didn't know if Quentin trying to come back was a message from God. Suppose God wanted us to be together? You know, that whole "what God has put together, let no man put asunder."

But finally, after a lot of prayer and a lot of patience from Brock, I cut all ties to Quentin and chose Brock.

He said, "When I'd wanted us to get back together, you asked me if I were gay, and I told you that I didn't need to label who I am or what I do."

"Except, we're all labeled."

"We shouldn't be. We should just be who we are."

"But it's confusing; are you bi, straight, or gay?"

He chuckled just a little. "You wanna know what I am?" He paused for just a moment. "I'm an American. An African American. An African-American man."

I shook my head. Quentin knew that wasn't good enough.

"Sheridan, whatever I call myself, that's my business. I'm the only one who matters."

"You...and Harmony."

"Let me worry about Harmony. Let me worry about living my life. That'll give you much more time to concentrate on living yours."

There was nothing that I could do except nod. I let a couple of moments pass by and then asked, "I just have to know...did I...did I turn you gay?"

His answer: He took a step closer, raised both his arms and after hesitating for just a second, he wrapped me in an embrace.

I just stood there with my arms at my side. But though I didn't hold him, I didn't push him away either. Instead, I was trying to figure it out, trying to feel the words that he wouldn't say.

After a couple of seconds, he stepped back, planted a soft kiss on my forehead, and then moved away and out of the kitchen without saying another word to me.

It wasn't until he released me that I realized I'd been holding my breath. I moved over to the counter, leaned against it, and listened as Quentin returned to the dining room.

"We've got to get going," he announced to everyone, and right away, chairs scraped against the floor. I could imagine them all rising, saying their goodbyes, and total sadness came over me. The Christmas that I thought was going to be bad had turned out exactly that way multiplied by one hundred.

Christopher and Tori...and Evon, too, were probably all furious with me. They would probably leave with Quentin.

But even though I wanted to go out there, say goodbye to Harmony, and beg my children to stay, I didn't move from the kitchen; I stayed away from that dining room.

So, I just waited, listening to the goodbyes, imagining the parting embraces. Even though I couldn't hear everything clearly, it didn't sound like anyone was sad. They were still chatting and laughing; there still seemed to be nothing but holiday cheer.

But that all could have been a trick, so I just stayed in place. The chime let me know that the front door had opened, though not even three minutes had passed since Quentin had walked out of the kitchen. Quentin, Harmony, and probably Christopher and Evon were all making a quick escape. Even Tori had probably tagged along with her brother, just to get away from her mother.

Sighing, I turned toward the stacked dishes, thinking that I might as well get the real cleanup started. As I opened the door to the dishwasher, I heard footsteps inching closer to the kitchen. I closed my eyes, not wanting to face my mother. But then, I decided to stand up and take my punishment like a woman.

When I turned around, I was a little surprised to see that it wasn't my mother who'd come for me; it was my husband.

Brock stood there, just watching me in silence for a moment, and I tried to hold his gaze, but I couldn't. I had to look away.

He moved toward me; then, he did what Quentin had done minutes before. He held me. This time, though, I raised my arms, and held him, too.

After a few moments, I asked, "Did everybody leave?"

He shook his head. "Just Quentin and Harmony."

"I wondered if Christopher and Evon had left."

He shook his head. "Nope; they're still here."

"I even worried about Tori."

"Where's she gonna go? She lives here."

"And Mom?"

"You know she's not leaving. She has the best bedroom in this house."

That made me laugh a little. "Thank you for not making me feel like a fool."

He shrugged. "You didn't need any help with that."

"Gee, thanks." I paused. "You know I love you, right?"

"That, I know."

Another moment, and then, "The questions I had...what was going on...none of it had anything to do with you, with us." I blew out a long breath that made me sound like I was exhausted. And I was. "I just had a few questions. All I wanted to know was..."

"If you had anything to do with him turning to a man," Brock finished my sentence for me.

I tilted my head. "Yes! So you knew that's what I was thinking?"

"Not the whole time, but it didn't take me long to figure it out. And really," he sighed, "I think any woman would wonder that after what happened between the two of you."

I nodded. "Truly, that's all it was. I didn't want you to think that..."

"You still love Quentin?" Again, he finished my thought for me. He shook his head. "No. I have no doubt about that. I know how much you love me."

I exhaled, so grateful that Brock knew the truth. "I'm glad."

"But you know you have to get over all of this, right?" He stared me down like a parent trying to make a point to a child. "We'll probably be around Quentin and Harmony again, and you'll always have questions, but..."

This time, I finished for him, "I need to keep my questions to myself."

He nodded. "This is his life, his choices, his decisions."

"I get it. I wish we'd had this talk before."

"Really, you and Quentin should've had this talk before he showed up to our home, with a fiancée, at Christmas."

"Yeah," I said with a little bit of a moan. "And then, maybe I wouldn't have ruined everyone's day."

"Who said you did that? Christopher, Tori, Evon, and your mom are waiting for us."

I frowned. "Waiting? For what?"

"We never opened our gifts."

My grin was immediate, and I clapped my hands. "Our gifts! This is how you know the children are grown. It's what...almost four o'clock and we haven't opened presents?"

"Nope. And that's how you know Christmas hasn't been ruined. Because the best part is still to come." He held out his hand, and I took just a moment to look at it before I hooked my fingers with his.

"Come on," he said, "let's go open some gifts."

He pulled me closer, kissed my cheek, and together we walked from the room.

And all I could think was that no matter what gifts waited for me under that tree, nothing would ever match the gift that I'd been given when I married Brock Eugene Goodman. Even with all that had gone down today, there was nothing but joy in my world.

My Christmas, Your Christmas, This Christmas

Kendall Leigh Stewart

Nine

stared into my coffee and watched the stream circle up to me. My eyes were bleary from my lack of sleep, and it took a tremendous effort for me to even lift my head. When I did, my eyes focused on the old-fashioned apple-shaped clock that had been hanging over the sink since I was a kid.

The hands on the clock had long ago rusted, but still the clock ticked and told the time: It was just about ten minutes to six.

Christmas morning had arrived.

It was almost as if I couldn't look away from the clock. And as I stared, I remembered. And as I remembered, I couldn't help but smile...

"Ssssh," I whispered to my little sister. "We can't wake them up yet, Sabrina. Not until six."

"Why not?" Sabrina whined. "Santa Claus left a long time ago. See," she picked up the saucer where our father had left three chocolate chip cookies the night before. Sabrina wouldn't go to bed until Santa's snacks had been set out. "And Santa put the glass in the sink, too. See," Sabrina said, pointing.

"Dang, that Santa sure is messy," I said picking up the glass. "Next time, he should wash it."

Sabrina shook her head. "He couldn't. He didn't have time because he had to take the reindeer all around the world."

I laughed and wondered if I'd been that gullible when I was five. I couldn't remember when I'd stop believing in Santa Claus, but whenever it was, now that I was twelve, I knew the whole truth. But I loved my baby sister too much to spoil it for her.

"Can we wake up Mama and Daddy now?"

Sabrina's whisper came out so loud, I put my hand over her mouth to quiet her down. "Sssh....we just have ten more minutes. It's almost six."

We tiptoed back to our bedroom, and I climbed into my bed. But right across from me, Sabrina sat on the edge of hers. "Is it time yet?" That was the question she asked me for the next nine minutes.

Finally, I nodded and Sabrina jumped up and dashed out of the room before I could even get my feet to hit the floor.

"Mama! Daddy! Santa came," Sabrina shouted as she ran down the hall. "You have to come and see!"

I had to shake my head a little to drag myself back to the present. The happiness that I'd felt on that Christmas morning and on the many Christmases that followed was supposed to last forever.

But the first sign that my forever was going to be short-lived was when my mother passed away five years later. And then after what happened with me, Sabrina and Anthony, Christmas became a holiday that was no longer to be celebrated with family. In fact, I spent most Christmases alone—though no one knew that. I always told my father that I was spending the holiday with friends. But in actuality, Christmas was just another workday for me.

Now though, with what my father told me the other day, this was a new Christmas; this was his Christmas.

So, I was going to do this, though it was going to be tough. Which is exactly why I stayed here with my dad last night. This way, there was no chance of me waking up this morning, getting in my car, and heading to San Diego or San Francisco or anyplace that wasn't Compton.

I had to smile a little bit at that thought. I could see myself in my convertible with the hood down and me speeding down Pacific Coast Highway. Maybe that's what I should've done. I glanced at the clock again; maybe I still had time to do it.

"No!" I scolded myself, even though I kept my eyes on that clock. I needed to be here, I needed to do this, and I could do it. I started my mantra all over again. "I can do this."

"I used to find your mother in here talking to herself just about every morning."

I shifted my glance from the clock to the doorway where my father stood. I was surprised; I usually heard my dad approaching as his slippers slid against the wooden tiles in the hallway. But I guess I'd been so deep in my thoughts, I hadn't heard him at all.

Without another word, he shuffled toward the counter, poured a cup of coffee, then sat down at the kitchen table with me. "You remind me so much of your mother, you know."

New memories came to my mind. Memories of my mother, the most beautiful mother in the world. I remembered being a teenager and watching *The Cosby Show*, and I'm telling you, I was sure that someone from NBC had come to our house and stolen a picture of my mom. She looked just like Clair Huxtable. But that was all that was left of my mother—the photos and the memories.

"Yup. I used to find your mother in here all the time." My father shook his head. "So many memories."

"Yeah. Memories everywhere in this house." My eyes swept through the kitchen. "Especially in here."

"Show me a home where the kitchen is the heart, and I'll show you a happy family." He chuckled. "We had good times, right here, right at this table."

I had to nod at that. "This is where I did my homework, where I learned how to sew."

"Where you learned how to cook."

"Not as good as Mama, though." I laughed. "But I tried."

"You certainly did, baby girl." He sighed, the sound filled with contentment. "Nothing but the best of memories, but I think some of my best memories are still to be made. They're in front of me."

I tilted my head and studied my father. "How do you do it, Daddy? How do you keep such a positive attitude in the midst of all of this?"

He shrugged. "It is what it is. None of us are gonna get out of life alive." He chuckled and the way he looked at me, it felt like he was waiting for me to join him.

But I didn't want to laugh...all I wanted to do was cry.

My father kept on, "It's easy for me to be positive. I know God's gonna work this thing out. If He does it on this side, I'll be given a few more years. If He does it on the other side, I know where I'm going, and I'm not afraid to get there. Either way, I'm gonna be healed. Plus," he paused for a moment, "whenever God calls me home, I have to say that I'm looking forward to seeing a few people."

A beat, and then, I said, "Mama?"

He nodded. "I don't know what heaven will be like. But I pray that I get the chance to tell Elena once again how much I love her and how sorry I am."

I did what I always did when my father talked about my mother this way—I kept my mouth shut. Because even though I was only seven years old when it happened, I was smart enough to understand that what happened was between my parents. And, I'd always been smart enough to leave it between my parents.

Of course when it happened, my heart broke for my mother. What daughter wouldn't feel sorrow, watching her mother cry for what seemed like months? Then, watching her finally accept her husband's apology for not only having an affair, but for bringing home the evidence of his infidelity after his Caucasian mistress and her family wanted nothing to do with the bronze-skinned child.

My father may have had a short-term affair, but it'd had long-term effects. My mother had agreed to raise her husband's child since the only other choice was foster care.

My mother had such a servant's soul, and I saw how hard she tried to love Sabrina. But with my young eyes, I could also see that every bit of love my mother gave to Sabrina broke my mother's heart just a little bit more until she had nothing left. And when it was all gone, she died—on her and my father's twentieth wedding anniversary.

My mother had left behind a husband, a stepdaughter, and a biological daughter who vowed that I would never suffer the pain that she did. I'd never give my heart away to anyone. I made that promise while standing over my mother's casket—that I would never get married.

"Yes," my father's voice came through my morbid memories. "I want the chance to tell your mother once again that I never meant to hurt her." And then he paused as if his words were some kind of set up. "Just like Anthony and Sabrina never meant to hurt you."

I sighed. "I'm so tired of hearing that, Daddy. But you know what? It doesn't even matter anymore. All that matters is you. This is your Christmas."

He chuckled. "This isn't my day; it belongs to all of us." My dad put down his cup and patted my hand. "I thank you for this, baby girl. I thank you for this one last holiday..."

"Don't say that, Daddy. Please don't say that."

He sat back and shook his head. "Don't you worry. I'm not gonna just accept this. Death ain't carrying me away without a fight."

"That's what I want to hear."

"But," he said, taking back the little bit of relief his words had just given me, "I also know the reality of it all. So, I'm ready. Whenever God calls me home, I'm ready. But you know what?" he added. "I don't want to talk about this today, all right? Today is all about celebration. Today, I'll have my two baby girls with me, and that's what's going to make me happy this Christmas."

I nodded and scooted my chair over a bit to get closer to my father. Then I leaned over and hugged him. "Merry Christmas, Daddy," I whispered.

"Merry Christmas, baby girl, Merry Christmas."

Ten

It was this moment that had kept me awake for most of the night. This moment when I would hear the car door slam and their footsteps coming toward the house.

But even though I'd thought about it for hours, I still didn't know what to do. Should I rise to greet them at the door? Or should I wait nonchalantly for them to come in, sitting as if I didn't care and hardly noticed their presence?

This was a big moment for me. I had to do it right. There was no doubt that Sabrina and Anthony were prepared for me because of Dad. So, I just wanted to be as ready for them.

As the faint footsteps on the brick walkway became louder and louder, I jumped up and scurried to the door. Decision made—I would do what I always did—I'd face my problems head on.

I whipped the door open, then stood there.

First up...my sister. My dad called me his baby girl, but Sabrina was his golden girl.

The last time I'd seen my sister this close, I'd tried to run her over with my car. I'd missed, of course. And frankly, perhaps murdering my sister wasn't exactly what I really wanted to do that day. She and Anthony hadn't been married yet, but they were certainly married now. And Sabrina had the bulging belly to prove that Anthony completely belonged to her.

"Hi, Kendall," Sabrina said with hesitation in her voice, but with a smile on her face that made her look like she was having a golden day.

My eyes were still on my sister's belly when I gave Sabrina my own version of hello, "You're pregnant."

In all the scenarios I'd imagined during the night, those words were not the first that I'd expected to say. I had wanted to be cool, collected, and clearly in charge in this moment. But what else was I supposed to say...I don't know why, but I was shocked.

Dad should've definitely told me about this. Not that I could really blame my father for not saying anything to me. He'd tried to share news of my sister with me all the time in the first few years, especially about her leukemia and how she'd gone into remission. But beyond her illness, whenever he brought her up, I did what I did best...I'd shut him down. And soon, my father just gave up.

But this...this was something that he should have insisted that I hear.

It wasn't until Sabrina leaned in and wrapped her arms around me that I realized my sister wanted a hug.

Really?

But today was Christmas.

I planted my feet, so that I couldn't jerk away, and then I reciprocated Sabrina's hug, giving my sister two quick taps on her back.

Sabrina's eyes shone brighter and her smile was wider when she stepped back. As if she was thrilled that I had actually almost hugged her—and hadn't hit her. "It really is good to see you," she said, sounding like she meant it.

I wasn't going to lie, not even with a smile. But I did manage to mumble, "Merry Christmas."

That seemed to be good enough for Sabrina as she moved aside.

And now, there was Anthony.

In the past six years, I'd had the opportunity to see Anthony a couple of times more than Sabrina. Two meetings, for the purpose of closing out our business partnership. Anthony had given me full ownership of the company we'd started together, the Women's Place—an upscale health club that provided fitness and beauty services—and I'd given Anthony our dream beach home in Malibu.

From the moment I'd discovered Sabrina in bed with my husband, Anthony had wanted our breakup to be amicable. So much so, that he actually had the audacity to invite me to their wedding. But since I called people who betrayed me enemies rather than friends, I wasn't interested in maintaining a relationship with the two people I'd once loved the most.

But maybe time...and fineness healed all wounds. Because now that Anthony stood in front of me, still looking like a super-size order of chocolate decadence, I didn't feel as bad as I thought I would.

"Merry Christmas, Kendall," he said with all that baritone in his voice.

He placed the two shopping bags he held against the wall, then reached out to pull me into his arms for a hug. His hug was different from my sister's. His hug lingered. It was a hug that was much more than I expected, much more than I wanted. But it wasn't awkward, not the way it had been with Sabrina. I kind of settled into Anthony's embrace, closed my eyes, inhaled the fragrance of his cologne, and remembered so much.

That was when I had to take a step back. I had to because it seemed that Anthony wasn't going to be the one to do it. When I looked up and into Anthony's eyes, I didn't find it as hard to smile.

"You're looking good, Kendall."

I knew that. I had gone through a lot of trouble to make sure. I'd stayed casual of course. My outfit, skinny jeans, with a hip-length white tank top, and loads of silver chains that matched my earrings and bracelets, was perfect for this extraordinarily warm Christmas Day. Only my above-the-knee brown stiletto boots gave any hint that it was winter.

But I'd always known that it was more than the clothes that made the woman. And that's why I worked out so much. Really, for the past six years, that's all I'd been doing—working and working out. My body and I were the best advertisement for The Women's Place. But to be honest, somewhere inside, I kinda felt like I'd been working out for this day, too. The day when Anthony would see me for the first time.

Anthony wore a smile, but besides that, I couldn't tell from his expression if his mind was filled with what ifs. But whether he had moments of regret or not, one thing was for sure—this was the first time in my life when I looked better than my giga-gorgeous sister. Of course, the major reason for that had to do with nature—Sabrina looked like she was minutes away from giving birth—everything from her face to her feet was swollen. But still, I was going to claim the victory any way I could get it.

"Yeah, you look really good," Anthony emphasized as if he wanted to make sure I'd heard him.

"You do look good," Sabrina said, closing the gap between her and her husband. She hooked her arm through Anthony's. "Dad's told us that you were doing well. And your business was, too. I hear women talking about The Women's Place everywhere I go." She paused and added. "I refer a lot of women there...to you..."

Sabrina left those words hanging in the air and I wondered what my sister wanted me to say. Thank you? It was difficult for me to give Sabrina any kind of thanks for anything while she was standing there holding onto Anthony.

So, I said nothing and motioned for Anthony and Sabrina to sit down. I directed them as if I was in charge, as if this were my place.

Anthony grabbed his shopping bags with gift-wrapped packages peeking over the top and shoved the bags under the tree. Then, in two seconds flat, he was back at Sabrina's side, helping her settle onto the sofa.

I snuggled into the worn chair across from them and studied the couple: how Anthony piled the pillows behind Sabrina's back and then waited until she nodded before he sat down.

For just an instant, I wondered how this scene would have played out if it were me and Anthony? I probably would have swatted him away—all that fussing over me when I could take care of myself.

But Sabrina seemed to relish it. And when Anthony sat down, he sat so close their bodies were almost one. Sabrina reached for his hand, and they held each other.

Now, I tried to imagine me sitting there with Anthony, but the only images that I could conjure up in my mind were me and Anthony in a boardroom. Truly, those were the only dreams I'd ever had for the two of us.

"So, Sabrina's right," Anthony said. "Dad has been keeping us abreast of all that's been going on with you."

My glance went right back to Sabrina's belly. "Well, he hasn't told me much about you two."

"That's because I felt that was something your sister should tell you."

The three of us looked up.

"Hi, Daddy!" Sabrina exclaimed, then moved as if she wanted to jump up. But she didn't make it all the way to her feet until Anthony stood beside her and hoisted her up. Then she rushed to our father, as if she'd never been so happy to see him.

I knew that my sister's enthusiasm wasn't just about greeting Dad on Christmas. Sabrina was probably just thrilled to have another ally in the room. That would make it three against one— to Sabrina, those odds were much more even.

Sabrina and Anthony greeted Dad, and I took in the laughter of the three as they exchanged Christmas good wishes, and hugs, and kisses. My father did a little quick boxing move with Anthony, and I marveled at just how effortlessly they moved together. Just like I did with him.

Of course, I knew that my father saw Sabrina and Anthony on the regular, but it wasn't until now that I thought about the three of them together. My dad had this whole other life with my sister. A life that included dinners and outings, birthdays and holidays. A life that was shared by a family. A life without me.

I wasn't complaining; this had been my choice. But all this time, I'd kinda believed that I was my father's only light. Clearly, though, I wasn't my father's only love.

Was that where the tug on my heart was coming from? Suddenly, I had this feeling that I'd missed out on so much.

"Okay, let's get you back on the couch," my dad said, finally breaking up their little family moment.

He reached for Sabrina's elbow, and my sister laughed. "Daddy, I'm just pregnant. You're treating me like I can't do anything."

"I don't care what you say," my dad said. "We're talking 'bout my first grandbaby here."

His words brought another tug to my heart. Sabrina was younger, yet she was going to be the one to give our dad probably the only earthly desire he had left. Especially now.

Once Sabrina was settled again, Dad sat next to me. "So, you're surprised about the baby, huh?" He grinned and patted my hand.

"Very."

"Well, like I said, I never said anything because that's something I wanted Sabrina to tell you." He paused. "I just think that there are some things sisters should share."

He left his words right there, as if that were a lesson for both of us.

Sabrina nodded as if she accepted what our father was trying to teach us. I didn't move.

Then, silence came and hovered over us like a low hanging cloud. I couldn't imagine that my dad, Sabrina, and Anthony had nothing to say. Maybe it was that my father, my sister, and my ex had plenty to say, but they just didn't want to say it in front of me. Silent seconds always seemed longer, and I wondered just how long this misery was going to last.

The sound of children's glee wafted through the windows, probably kids out on the streets showing off their new Christmas toys: tricycles, bicycles, and skateboards. But the sounds of Christmas were all outside. There was not a bit of the gaiety of the day inside these four walls.

When no one spoke up, I raked through my mind for something to say. But all that came out, though, was, "So, how's the house?"

Sabrina and Anthony exchanged a look. Then, Anthony said, "We sold the house. Not too long after..."

When he stopped, I raised my eyebrows. Why was he hesitating? So, I said it for him. "Your wedding?"

He nodded.

"You could have said that." I waved my hand in the air as if none of this was a big deal. "We're all grownups; after what happened between us, we should be able to talk about anything. Trust me, after finding your sister screwing your husband in your bed, there's nothing..."

"Kendall!"

"No, Daddy. Let me finish. I'm just saying no one has to tiptoe around me 'cause I'm surely not gonna tiptoe around anyone."

"We did sell the house after we got married," Sabrina spoke up, as if it would be better to talk about it and get it over with. "Because I didn't want to live there. It didn't feel like I should be there. It felt like I'd taken that from you."

My mouth opened wide. I'm telling you, if it could have, my jaw would've been on the floor. But no words came out of me, only laughter. I leaned back and howled as if Sabrina's statements were the funniest lines I'd ever heard. I laughed so hard, tears began to flow.

But then, when I looked up, I was surprised that I was the only one laughing. "I'm sorry," I said. "I just can't believe you said that."

The three of them stared at me like I was having some kind of breakdown.

So I broke it down for them. "You felt like you were taking the house from me?" I said, looking straight at my sister. "You're a little mixed up, Sabrina. You *took* my husband; I *gave* you the house."

"Kendall!" my father snapped again.

"Okay," I held up her hands, surrendering. "I'm sorry. It's just that..."

"Can we change the subject?" my father pleaded.

"Sure," I said. But it was tough to sit there because every time I looked over at Sabrina, I wanted to bust out laughing again.

So I just looked down at my hands as more seconds ticked by. Sabrina placed her hands on her belly and lowered her eyes. Anthony found something of interest outside the window, and my father moved between glancing at me, then looking away and shaking his head.

It was only because of my father that I wished I could take back my words. Even though all I'd been trying to do was help to get some kind of conversation started, I had to do better.

So, I tried again. "I have an idea."

Three pairs of eyes shot to me—all wide and filled with horror, as if I'd just pulled a gun on them.

"No, really," I said quickly, trying to assuage all of their fears. "I have an idea. A good idea. Let's open the gifts."

Collectively, they exhaled. And the cloud of disaster that hovered low and close, lifted.

Sabrina said, "That is a good idea, but do we want to do it so early?"

For a moment, I was taken back again to Christmases of decades past. When for Sabrina, it was never too early to open presents.

Sabrina kept on, "I mean, I was thinking after dinner." Then she looked at me and added quickly, "But if you want to open gifts now..."

"Yes, let's do it." My father shifted to the edge of his seat. "Sister Henderson said she'd bring dinner over about four."

I glanced at my watch. Good grief! That was almost two hours from now. How would we fill up all of that time?

Yes, we needed to open gifts...very slowly. And then, I needed to call Sister Henderson, the woman who'd been preparing special dinners for my father for all the years since my mother had been gone, and offer to triple pay her if she could get that turkey and dressing over here an hour earlier than planned.

"Okay," Sabrina said. "Then let's do the gifts." Her eyes twinkled with excitement, as if she were six years old once again. "I just have to send this one text," she added.

"Who you texting, baby?" Anthony asked.

"Just someone from the office," Sabrina said, already texting. It took her no longer than ten seconds before she said, "Alright, let's do this."

"I'll get the gifts." I jumped up and knelt under the tree before any of them could offer to help. I needed to do something with my hands so that my tongue would stay silent.

There were only four boxes, and they were all tagged with my dad's name. That's what I expected. I didn't know what Sabrina and Anthony did, but Dad and I hadn't exchanged Christmas gifts for years. My thoughts: my father didn't need to be spending his money on me, and really, I tried to make every day Christmas for my dad in some way.

"These are all for you, Daddy," I said, as I stacked the packages one on top of the other, then placed the gifts at my father's feet.

Dad rubbed his palms together and grinned. "Well, Merry Christmas to me!"

For the first time, we all laughed at the same time.

I settled back in my chair and watched my father brighten with joy. But then, I felt a shadow over me; it was Anthony.

"Merry Christmas," he said, holding a box. I stared at it for a moment, then glanced up at him, before my eyes returned to the box. The box and Anthony took me back in time. Back to our first Christmas...

Even though I had on a sweatshirt and jeans, my feet were bare as I perched them up on the deck's railing. Although the ocean breeze was cool, the hot chocolate warmed me up. I took a small sip and then sighed.

This was the life! We didn't have a bit of money, but I felt like I had everything that money could buy. I had the business that had started formulating in my head when I was a freshman in college, and I was living in a Malibu home that I couldn't even have imagined when I was growing up on the hard streets of Compton.

Yup, I had everything.

"Good morning."

I glanced over my shoulder and smiled at Anthony standing at the sliding glass door. Oh, yeah...I had a husband, too. Not that Anthony was really an afterthought. It was just that to me, he was part of the business. When we'd met in graduate school, he was the one who encouraged me, planned with me, and then helped me make my dream come true.

"Good morning," I said. "Merry Christmas."

He stepped onto the deck and kissed my cheek. "Merry Christmas to you." He sat down in the deck chair lined up next to mine. "What time should we head over to your father's?"

I sighed. "I wish we could just spend our first Christmas here, looking out onto the ocean."

Anthony chuckled just a bit. "Your father would never go for that."

"I know. And neither would Sabrina. My little sister would drive over here and drag me back over there." I laughed, and then sighed. "I just want a few more minutes here. And then I'll get ready."

"Okay, but before we do that..." He paused and pulled a box from the pocket of the sweat suit that he wore. "Merry Christmas."

My mouth opened wide. "Oh, my goodness. I didn't expect this." Looking up at him, I added, "And I didn't get anything for you."

He held up his hand. "That's okay. I didn't give it to you so that I could get a gift in return." He nodded. "I saw this in the store the other day and thought of us. Go ahead, open it."

I hesitated because I felt so bad. This was our first Christmas together, and I swear, I didn't even think about buying Anthony a gift. I hadn't bought anyone anything. But now that I was sitting here in this moment, I guess I should have gotten my husband something.

"Go ahead," Anthony said once again.

I flipped the cover off the box and gasped. "This is beautiful," I said as I pulled out the silver half-heart charm that hung on a chain.

Anthony said, "I have the other half." He pulled down the high collar of his sweatshirt and showed me the other half of the heart hanging from a chain around his neck.

"We are two halves to one whole," he said as I sat up so that he could secure the chain around my neck. Then he wrapped his arms around me from behind. "My heart doesn't beat without you."

I wanted to say those words back to him, but I couldn't. I wanted to feel exactly the way he felt, but I didn't. I loved Anthony, I did. Because of all that he'd done for me. But the sentimental stuff—I'd been trying, but it just wasn't in me. I wanted to, but every time I thought about giving my heart to Anthony, I thought about my mother...and my father...and my mother's heart...and my mother's death.

But I had to find a way to stop making the sins of my father the sins of every man. All men were not the same. All men didn't cheat.

I massaged the silver heart that my husband had just given me. And with his arms around me, I made a silent promise to Anthony. I was going to try. From this Christmas forward I was going to try to be his loving wife. I was going to try to find a way to give my heart to him.

Leaning back into Anthony's arms, I rested against his chest. "I love you, Anthony," I said to him.

I felt him stiffen a bit with surprise because I'm sure he could count the number of times I'd said those words. But then, he relaxed and held me tighter. "I love you, too, baby. Merry Christmas."

I smiled, knowing that I'd just given my husband the best Christmas gift, the only gift that he wanted from me...

"This is from me and Sabrina," Anthony said, making me blink my way back to 2013.

He was still holding the box out in front of me, and it took a couple of seconds for my brain to comprehend it. A gift? For me? From them?

"Uh...thank you." I took the box, wondering if I were supposed to tell them that I hadn't spent a nickel nor a dime to get them anything. "I didn't..."

Anthony held up his hand, just like he did on that Christmas morning so long ago. "No problem," he said, as if he knew what I was going to say. "We," he glanced over at Sabrina, "wanted to do this for you."

So what was I supposed to do now? Open it? Or wait?

Then Sabrina helped me make the decision. "Open it," she said, sounding once again like she was six. "I hope you like it."

Slowly, I unwrapped the box, starting at each of the ends, pulling the paper apart gently as if I planned to use the gift wrap again. The size of the box made it hard to keep my thoughts away from the past. This was just like the box that Anthony had given me back then.

I lifted the top of the box and gasped.

"You like it!" Sabrina exclaimed. "I'm so glad."

It took a moment for me to lift up the chain with a heart, a full heart this time, that dangled at the end. Another heart? From Anthony?

Then Sabrina explained, "I saw this in the store the other day and thought of us." Her words were eerie, just like the words Anthony had said back at our first Christmas. "Do you see the inscription?"

I turned the heart over in my hand: *A sister is a gift to the heart.* My eyes stayed on the words, reading them over again. And then, I felt that tug on my heart again. I knew what it was this time. Something was trying to pull me away from my anger. But I wasn't going to fall for the sentiment.

It wasn't until I heard my sister's voice that I looked up.

"I really mean that," Sabrina whispered. Now she was the one standing over me. I hadn't even noticed that she'd stood up.

Sabrina continued, "No matter what has happened, you've always been a gift from God to my heart." With her big belly and all, she leaned over and hugged me. "Merry Christmas, Sis."

Just as I lifted my arms to hug my sister back, to wrap her in an embrace for the first time in more than six years, the doorbell rang, and I jumped away from Sabrina and out of the chair. That doorbell felt like a save that had come directly from heaven.

"I'll get it." I rushed to the door, praying that Sister Henderson was on the other side, hours early with our dinner.

I pulled open the door, and a second after that, my mouth stretched wide with surprise. "Oh, my god!"

Sabrina had been right behind me, and she rushed through the door.

"I didn't think you were gonna get here on time," Sabrina said. Then, with a grin, she turned back and pulled him inside. "And now, here is my Christmas gift to everyone!"

He stepped over the threshold.

"Hey, everybody, Merry Christmas!"

"Oh, my god," I said again, as I wrapped my arms around his neck. "What are you doing here, D'Angelo?"

Now, this was a man that I wanted to hug.

He grinned when he stepped back. "It's good to see you again, Kendall."

"D'Angelo!" my dad exclaimed. He pushed himself up and moved to the door to greet him. "Man, it's so good to see you. How many years has it been?"

D'Angelo shrugged. "I don't know. Too long, though."

Finally, D'Angelo turned to Anthony. The two stared at each other for a long moment before D'Angelo reached out. "How you doing, lil bro? How you doin'?"

He embraced his brother, but from where I stood, I could see that Anthony's reaction to D'Angelo's hug was the same as my reaction had been to Sabrina's; he barely touched his brother.

I folded my arms and leaned against the door. Sister Henderson could take her time because I had no doubt there would be plenty of conversation now. Christmas had just become very, very interesting.

Eleven

"So come on over here and sit down," my father said once D'Angelo stepped back and away from Anthony. "My, my, my, this is a great Christmas gift." He led D'Angelo to the chair where I had been sitting.

But I didn't mind. I had the best seat in the house. I stood, leaning against the wall near the door, feeling like an observer outside of the circle. Exactly where I wanted to be.

"So, are you just getting back in the country, or have you been here for a while?" my father asked.

"I just got back in from Iraq last night, Sir. I decided to come home after I heard from Sabrina."

"Sabrina?" Anthony piped in. His eyes moved from his brother to his wife. "You two've been in touch?" he addressed Sabrina.

"Yes," she said. "We've been talking through email."

Wow, that was a bold move. Talking to Anthony's brother without Anthony knowing it?

"And a couple of times on Skype," D'Angelo added.

I could tell by the way my sister bit the edge of her lip that she wished D'Angelo had kept that part of their communication to himself.

"Emails? Skype? Why were you guys even talking?" Anthony asked.

"I wanted him to know about the baby," Sabrina said quickly, and she placed her hand over her husband's. Only I seemed to notice the way Anthony slipped his hand away from Sabrina.

Sabrina explained some more, "I wanted him to know that he was gonna be an uncle."

I wondered if I were the only one who could feel my ex-husband's rage. Was it because we'd been married? Or was it because now I, too, felt rage?

Sabrina had contacted D'Angelo, who was halfway around the world, to tell him about her baby. Yet, she hadn't dialed the ten digits of a local number to call her sister? Hell, I would've appreciated even an email.

"So, how is it over there?" my dad asked.

D'Angelo shook his head. "The same. It's tough. Still unstable."

"But you're not in the military, right?" he asked. Before D'Angelo could answer, my father added, "For the life of me, I can't figure out why anyone would go over there if they didn't have to. What were you doing over there, Son?'"

D'Angelo paused for a moment, then said with a smile, "Well, Sir, I was making an honest living, but that's all I can say." A beat. "'Cause if I tell you, then I'll have to kill you."

Another beat, and then my dad leaned back and laughed. A hearty laugh, a cleansing laugh, a laugh that I hadn't heard from my father in a while.

Sabrina chuckled along, but Anthony didn't. And all I did was smile. D'Angelo may have been trying to present it as a joke, but I had a feeling that what he said wasn't that far from the truth.

D'Angelo was a bad boy from way back; he still wore his gangster swag like a designer suit.

He'd been back and forth between the US and Iraq since 2003, and from what I'd been able to piece together, he worked for some kind of militia; his was a private group, not sanctioned by the government. So, I was sure that D'Angelo meant what he said when he told my father that he couldn't share secrets. He lived on that kind of edge.

D'Angelo had been living like that for all the years that I'd known him, and for the many years before. Every time I was in the same room with this man, I was fascinated.

Two years older than Anthony, the brothers were as different as the East was from the West. While Anthony was a straitlaced, live by the law, live by the book kind of guy, D'Angelo didn't believe that there was a rule or a law written that applied to him.

According to Anthony, it was that thinking that had landed D'Angelo in juvenile detention centers for short stints several times before he was even sixteen. But he was bright, a superior athlete, and with the help of his parents, who were both teachers, and his high school guidance counselor who saw his potential, D'Angelo excelled his last two years in high school.

It was in high school where I met D'Angelo. Well, I didn't exactly meet him; actually, I didn't know him at all. I was just a freshman, he was a junior, and my girlfriends and I would be in awe every time we saw D'Angelo and his boys pimp-strutting through the halls of Compton High. It was funny to me later when I found out Anthony was in the same school; we were in the same grade. But I never noticed him at all. All the air was taken up by his brother.

After D'Angelo graduated, he attended the University of California at Berkeley, and the college years allegedly calmed him down. He ended up graduating with honors and tried his hand as a salesman in corporate America, first as a salesman for IBM, and then a pharmaceutical salesman.

But I guess old ways die hard because soon selling legal drugs had led to selling legal drugs illegally. And from what I heard, D'Angelo had moved up in the streets pretty fast. He was living large, well-respected, and always two steps ahead of the law. I always believed that it was D'Angelo's legal businesses (real estate, small business investments) that kept him off the radar. That, and a couple of cops on his payroll. He was even known around Compton as a philanthropist.

After high school, I never saw D'Angelo again. Just heard his name here and there, so I was shocked the day Anthony took me to his home, and D'Angelo was there. The teenage crush that I'd had came rushing back. But I was smart enough to know that it was only a crush. Plus by then, Anthony was really into me and I...was really into the business plan that Anthony and I were putting together.

"The whole region is still recovering from the US invasion."

D'Angelo's voice brought me back, and as he talked to my dad, I crouched down and sat on the floor with my back against the wall and my knees pulled to my chest. I just sat there and listened as the conversation flowed easily between my dad and D'Angelo, with an occasional question from Sabrina. It was only those three who spoke; Anthony and I didn't say a word.

They'd been talking for about an hour when my father said, "Wait a minute; you've been here all this time, and I haven't offered you anything to drink. You want something?"

"Maybe just a glass of water," D'Angelo said.

Before my father could stand, I did. "I'll get it for you." I asked, "Does anyone else want anything?"

When my dad, Sabrina, and Anthony shook their heads, I moved toward the kitchen, grabbed a glass from the cabinet, and when I turned around, D'Angelo was standing right behind me.

"I would've brought this to you," I said.

"Why would I let you bring this to me when this will give me a couple of minutes to spend just with you?"

I tilted my head just a little. Was he flirting with me? And then I pushed that thought right out of my mind. No, he was just doing what bad boys did. He talked to all women this way. Every conversation was a flirtation. I held the glass up to the dispenser on the refrigerator, filled it with water, then handed it to him.

He took the glass, sipped, and said, "I was really sorry to hear about you and my brother." He glanced over his shoulder and made a motion with his head toward the living room. "What the two of them did to you, that was foul."

"So they told you?" I asked. I folded my arms and leaned against the counter.

"No, *they* didn't." He swallowed the rest of the water. "Sabrina did." Resting the glass in the sink, he asked, "So, even with all of that, you guys are cool?"

Sabrina obviously hadn't told D'Angelo everything, and I wasn't about to explain the real reason why I was here. Whatever my dad wanted D'Angelo to know, he'd have to tell him himself. So all I said was, "Cool is not exactly the word I'd used. But we try...mostly for my father, you know."

He nodded. "Yeah. I've always liked your dad. He's cool people." He stood next to me, mimicked my stance, and leaned back against the counter. "So you haven't remarried?"

I shook her head. "Nope. I've been too busy with life, with my business. Haven't had too much time."

Then he did that thing that all bad boys seemed to do. With hooded eyes, he looked me up, then he looked me down, and then he did it again. "You sure've been doing something, 'cause you look good!"

I laughed, though I was filled with a couple of other emotions, too. Like, how uncomfortable D'Angelo was making me feel; but how at the same time, I kinda liked it.

It had been a long time since any man had shown me any kind of attention. Or maybe I should correct that and say it had been a long time since I noticed. After Anthony, I'd decided that getting married had been a bad move, and I wasn't going to try again.

But this right here, standing with D'Angelo, felt...interesting.

"You know," D'Angelo said and then he leaned a little closer. "My brother's loss is going to be another very, very, very lucky man's gain."

He was so close to me now that his breath heated my skin. He was so close that surely he could feel my heart beat.

"Excuse me!"

At the sound of Anthony's voice, I jumped away from D'Angelo, leaping to the other side of the kitchen. But D'Angelo didn't move an inch. He just lifted his head, turned to his brother, and grinned.

"What's up, bro? Me and Kendall were just catching up."

Anthony glared at his brother, and before a fight broke out, I asked him, "Did you want something?"

"Uh...no. When you didn't come back, I wondered...yeah, I want a glass of water." Anthony marched to the cabinet, got his own glass, filled it with water, and just stood there.

I expected him to take his glass back with him into the living room. But he made it clear; he wasn't going anywhere.

I could actually feel the air, it was so thick, but it seemed like I was the only one who noticed. Because Anthony just stood there glaring at his brother, and D'Angelo just stood there, chuckling at Anthony.

Since I wasn't going to be able to stop whatever was going to go down between the two of them, I made a move to leave them alone. But before I stepped out of the kitchen, I said, "Remember, it's Christmas."

I didn't get two feet out of the kitchen, though, when the doorbell rang. I glanced up at the clock—just a little before four.

"That's our dinner," I said, thinking that this was another bell-saving moment. It would at least put the all-out battle I felt brewing between the brothers on hold.

When I rushed out of the kitchen, D'Angelo followed behind me. My father got to the door before I did.

"Sister Henderson," my dad greeted the woman. "Merry Christmas."

"Same to you, Brother Leigh." She lugged in a sagging pan that looked like it was filled with a twenty-pound turkey. "The rest of the food is in the backseat of the car," she said as she traipsed through the house.

My dad and D'Angelo jogged down the three steps to the walkway just as Sabrina pushed herself from the sofa. "I'm going to go to the bathroom before we sit down to eat," she announced.

As my father and D'Angelo came back into the house, Sister Henderson and I took the dishes from them and lined them onto the serving table in the dining room.

"Now, if y'all are gonna eat right away, we won't have to worry about heating any of this good food up," Sister Henderson said.

"Ma'am, may I just say that I'm ready to eat right now," D'Angelo said. "This looks so good."

"This young man has been over in Iraq," my dad explained. "He ain't seen food like this in months."

As Sister Henderson chatted with the two men, I decided that this would be my moment to escape. The way that food looked, the way I planned to eat, I needed to get comfortable. My plan was to go into the bedroom, kick off my boots, and slide into my slippers.

But right as I got outside of my bedroom, I stopped. It was the hushed voices that made me press my back against the hallway wall, then tilt my head so that I could hear.

"I can't believe you did that, Sabrina," Anthony whispered. "You know how I feel about him."

"With our baby coming, I just thought we needed to fix all of that. We've got to get this family right." Sabrina's voice was as low as his.

"You haven't been talking about fixing anything with Kendall."

"Are you kidding me? I've wanted to fix things with my sister since forever."

"Yeah, well, you haven't made much of an effort."

"Look, Anthony..."

"No, you look. I don't want to have anything to do with D'Angelo, and you know that. But you didn't care about my feelings. You were just gonna try to force it."

"He's your brother; he's family. And that makes him worth fighting for."

"Why? Why should I fight for a relationship with the one person who's responsible for my parents' death."

"He's not responsible for that. It was an accident, and I can't believe that you're still saying that."

"It wasn't an accident!" Anthony growled. "You know what people on the street are saying."

"People on the street? Really? Years later and you're still listening to people on the street? Why not listen to the police?"

"'Cause I know what I know."

There was a little bit of a pause and then, "Anthony, you've got to find a way to get over this."

"Don't you dare tell me to do that," he said, raising his voice a bit. "I lost my parents!"

I turned my head to see if my father or D'Angelo had heard the uprise. But when all I heard was their laughter in the dining room with Sister Henderson, I turned my focus back to Sabrina and Anthony.

His voice was low again when he said, "I will never sit down with that man."

I couldn't see, but Anthony must've turned away because Sabrina yelled out, "Where are you going?"

"I just told you. I'm getting out of here."

"We can't do that. What about dinner? What about my father?"

"If you cared about your father, if you cared about me, you wouldn't have invited my brother."

"Okay, I'm sorry, I was just trying to put everything back together, and with what's going on with Dad, I thought this would be the perfect time for all of us to reconcile."

"Well, you were wrong."

"So you're just gonna leave?"

"Yeah. But you can stay if you want to. I'm out."

"No, wait. You can't just leave. What are we gonna say to my father? You know how important this Christmas is to him."

"Alright, you want me to stay? You think that will be better? You think me and D'Angelo sitting down at the table and me prodding him to finally tell the truth about who blew up my parents' car...you think that's what your father wants at Christmas?"

"It doesn't have to be that way," Sabrina breathed. "We could all sit down and just talk like family. Today's not supposed to be about death. Today is supposed to be only about life."

"I can't give you that, Sabrina. So I'll make some excuse and get out of here."

"Well, then, I'm going with you."

I could hear the tears in my sister's voice and for just the smallest of moments, I felt sorry for her. It had been almost ten years since Anthony and D'Angelo's parents had died in what most said was a freak accident. The engine in their car had started smoking while they were on the 405 freeway. The reports had shown that while Anthony and D'Angelo's father was trying to ease to the shoulder, he'd cut in front of an eighteen wheeler that rammed into his Honda, crashing the car into the back of another truck. It ended up being a five-car pileup with two fatalities—their parents.

But Anthony never believed the police report. He'd heard some people talking, saying that what happened to his parents was payback for some long ago deal that had gone bad with D'Angelo and some other dealers. But even after an investigation that supported the original report, from the bottom of his heart, Anthony swore that he was the only one on earth who knew the truth—not counting the guys on the street, of course.

I'd always wondered why he'd wanted to believe that his brother was responsible for their parents' death. But with D'Angelo away so much, and the brothers half-estranged, I never brought him up.

Clearly though, my sister had tried a different approach.

"I'll just tell Daddy that I'm not feeling well," I heard Sabrina say. There was a pause and then, "Please, don't say anything else. I don't want to ruin the rest of the day for him."

In the silence of the next seconds, I figured that they were moving toward the door and with two hops, I jumped inside the bathroom. The door was barely closed before Anthony and

Sabrina walked by. I'd kept it open just enough so that I could watch them pass, then I stepped out, following them.

I entered the dining room just as Sabrina said, "I'm so sorry...but, I'm not feeling well."

"Oh, sweetheart, what's wrong?" The smile that had been on my father's face for the last couple of hours faded away. And now, his forehead creased with deep lines.

"I don't know," Sabrina said, looking down and away from our father. "Maybe I'm overdoing it, and I don't want to take a chance with the baby." She placed her hands over her belly.

"Maybe you should lie down."

She shook her head and finally looked up at Dad. Tears were in her eyes when she glanced over at Anthony. "No, I think it would be best if I went home." Facing our father again, she said, "I'm sorry, Daddy. I just ruined your Christmas."

"No, golden girl." He put his arms around her. "You could never ruin anything. I need you to be okay; I need you to take care of my first grandbaby." He leaned back. "Did you hear what I said?" he asked, trying to make her smile. "I said my first grandbaby. That means I expect you and Anthony to give me a whole lot more. And, I'm gonna be around to meet all of them."

Now, she embraced him. "Daddy, I'm so, so sorry," she sobbed.

"What you sorry about, golden girl? Don't worry about me. This was already a great day. I had my two girls here," he said, glancing at me. "And D'Angelo is home. This has been a wonderful Christmas."

"All right," Anthony said, finally speaking up. "I'm gonna get her home."

"Do you guys want to fix a couple of plates to take with you?" Dad asked.

Sabrina shook her head, and Anthony said, "No, suddenly I'm not hungry." Then, he glanced straight at his brother before he turned to me. His eyes were on me when he said, "Dad, would you mind helping Sabrina to the car? There's something I want to do."

"Sure," my father said, so unaware of the lies and the tension that weighed heavy in the air.

Anthony said nothing until my father and Sabrina were in the living room. "Kendall, can I see you in the kitchen?"

I frowned. I'd thought that Anthony was staying behind to talk to D'Angelo. What did he want with me? And whatever he wanted, why couldn't he talk to me where I was standing?

But I was curious enough to find out. As I moved toward the kitchen, I glanced back at D'Angelo, who was leaning against the serving table with his arms crossed and an expression of total amusement on his face. He chuckled as I shrugged.

Inside the kitchen, I crossed my arms. "What do you want?"

"I want you to stay away from my brother."

I opened my mouth, but nothing came out. It was the audacity and the absurdity of his words that shocked me into silence. But then, I got it together and said, "Do you want to repeat that?" Before he opened his mouth, I held up my hand. "And before you do that, think about you're saying."

He pressed his lips together hard as if he really did want to repeat what he said.

"That's what I thought." I rolled my eyes, and turned away.

But then, Anthony said, "Look, all I'm saying is that my brother is bad news. And, I don't think it's a good idea for you to spend time with him."

I laughed, and then I stopped. And when I stopped, I moved back over to him and got right in Anthony's face. "You don't have the right to tell me anything," I said. "You gave all of that up when you slept with my sister."

If it weren't Christmas and if I didn't think that my dad would be coming back at any moment, I would've stayed right there and had a knock-down drag-out with Anthony. But really, there was no need for that because I'd said what I needed to say. I'd summed it up in that one sentence.

By the look in his eyes—a cross between hurt and anger—I didn't need to say any more. I marched back into the dining room, and then just because I was sure that Anthony was going to make one final stop in there, I walked right up to D'Angelo and hugged him.

"I'm really glad you're back," I said.

I was pretty sure that D'Angelo knew my game, and he played along. He hugged me tightly, and then after a couple of seconds, he whispered in my ear, "He's gone."

I leaned away from him. "Thank you."

"You really gave it to my brother."

"That's not what I was trying to do."

He laughed. "Yeah, right. But no problem. I don't mind being used."

"I wasn't using you. I really am glad that you're back and that you're here and that you're having dinner with us. Especially now that Sabrina and Anthony are gone."

"Well, with all of this good food, I'm glad to be here."

"Good! Then that means that you, me, and my dad will have a great Christmas."

He nodded, then pulled one of the chairs out from the table. "Your seat, Miss."

"Thank you, Sir."

Right at that moment, my dad strolled back into the dining room. "Well, they're off," he said. "I was a little worried about Sabrina, but once Anthony got in the car, she seemed to feel better. I think she just needs to rest."

"Well then, Mr. Leigh, if she's okay, let's get this merry Christmas started."

My father smiled and reached for my hand. I took his and D'Angelo's, and we lowered our heads as Dad blessed the food. After that, I stood up and served the men, something I hadn't done in years, but something that made me feel so good today.

As we sat and ate and chatted, I marveled at how just a few hours ago, I thought this was going to be such a dreadful day. But this had turned into one of those merry little Christmases that I used to have.

"So, how long are you going to be in Los Angeles, D'Angelo?" my father asked, just as I stood up to clear the dinner plates away so that we could get to the dessert.

He swallowed a couple of sips of his iced tea, then said, "I'm not sure yet." He was speaking to my father, but then D'Angelo looked at me. "I was thinking a couple of weeks or so, unless...something comes up and I have to stay longer."

Now, I didn't have a single reason to believe that D'Angelo was talking about me. Except for the way he was looking at me in that bad boy kind of way, like I was a premium piece of filet mignon.

Like I said, it had been years...and it just felt good.

I hid my smile as I turned and carried the dishes into the kitchen. As I passed through the walkway, I glanced into the living room and what caught my eye? The mistletoe.

I couldn't help it—I smiled. And I couldn't help it when I began singing under my breath, "Hang all the mistletoe. I'm gonna get to know you better...this Christmas..."

Some Holy Night

Asia Ingrum

Twelve

I rested my hands on the steering wheel, lowered my head, and began my mantra all over again. "I can do this. I can do this."

"Mom!"

Then came the knocking on the window.

I raised my head, and there was Angel's face pressed against the window. "Get out the car, Mom,'" she demanded as if she were the adult.

And then, as if I were the child, I shook my head and started the ignition. I was gonna get up out of here.

"Mom!" Angel's shriek was so loud it sounded like she was inside the car with me.

"Okay, okay!" All I wanted to do was drive straight away. This couldn't be a good idea. No matter how I looked at it. But for my child's sake, I turned off the engine, opened the door, and then stepped outside like a big girl.

"I can do this," I said to Angel.

My daughter's sympathetic smile broke my heart. I wished that I could be stronger for her.

"Yes, you can," she said to me, in an encouraging tone that sounded much wiser than her eleven years. "It's not going to be that bad. Remember, Dad loved you once."

"And while he was loving me, his wife was hating me," I reminded her. My daughter was fully aware of the good, the bad, and the ugly of my relationship with her father. She knew that she was here because of an affair. And she knew she was here because she was so loved.

"Well, she doesn't hate you anymore. She's the one who invited you."

I gave my daughter a sideways glance. "You know that's not true. You know this was all your father."

"Well, even if it was his idea at first, Mom Caroline agreed," Angel insisted.

I cringed again. There was that Mom Caroline. No matter how many years I would be given on this earth, I was never going to accept that name for Bobby's wife.

My daughter took my hand and led me as if I didn't know the way. But I did. I'd been inside this mansion before—twice. Both times, I'd come to see Bobby's wife.

The first time was right after Bobby had told me that our ten-year love affair was over. If Bobby had thought I was going to go away quietly, he hadn't known the woman that he'd called his wife-on-the-road very well.

My game plan was to come here and shock his wife. I'd been so sure that once Caroline heard about her husband's long term affair and the daughter we'd had together, Caroline would cry hysterically, pack her bags, and move right back to Dallas, taking her bleeding heart with her.

But it didn't go down that way. I'd been the one who'd been cut to the core when Caroline told me that she'd known about our affair all along.

I'll never forget when she said: *Now that his playing days are over, Bobby and I have agreed that his playin' days are over. All the groupies and the hos have to go.*

Caroline had played *me*. She was the one calling the shots; she was the one who shut down my affair with Bobby.

So, that had been a devastating day, but it was nowhere as scary as when I'd had to come back and ask Caroline for her help. I'm telling you, I had to almost drop to my knees to convince her to stop Bobby from going after sole custody of Angel. And she'd come through.

Still, I couldn't figure out why I agreed to this. It was always stupid for the mistress to show up at the home of the wife. Always.

But then, my reason for being here squeezed my hand. "Mom, you okay?"

I nodded.

In front of the massive wooden doors, Angel said, "You can do this."

I inhaled, exhaled, and nodded again.

"And thanks, Mom. Thanks for doing this for me. Thanks for coming so that we could spend Christmas together." She kissed my cheek. "Merry Christmas, Mommy."

"Merry Christmas, baby," I said.

Angel was my reason. That's what I had to keep in mind. No matter what happened once we stepped into this house, it was all about my daughter.

Angel pushed opened the heavy door as if she lived there. And then, I remembered—my daughter did live in this house every other weekend, on some holidays, and half of her summer vacation.

The moment she stepped over the threshold, Angel shouted, "Mom, Dad, I'm home."

Mom? Now Mom Caroline didn't sound so bad.

But even as Angel called out again, I doubted that anyone could hear her. There were so many people, moving back and forth, and the music—some kind of classical rendition of "O Holy Night" seemed to be coming from invisible overhead speakers.

I stood there for a moment taking in the scene. This palatial entryway seemed grander than I remembered. The eight-foot Christmas tree standing between the twin winding staircases didn't even look like it was taking up much room—that's how big this space was. All around us, people chatted, laughed, and drank.

"Angel!" I hissed and grabbed my daughter's wrist just as she was about to jump into the crowd. "What is this? Some kind of party?"

"No, Mom," Angel laughed. "Not a party. Just Christmas dinner. This is how Dad and Mom Caroline do it for every holiday. They had almost fifty people here for Thanksgiving dinner."

Fifty people?

"Dad said that today there're gonna be about one hundred people because of Grandma and Grandpa's anniversary."

Who throws a party like this on Christmas?

"Sweetheart!"

Both Angel and I turned at the sound of Bobby's voice.

"Hi, Daddy," Angel squealed as she leapt into his arms. Then, "Mom Caroline, Merry Christmas," she giggled as she wrapped her arms around her stepmother.

I didn't even notice Bobby's wife because my eyes stayed on Bobby. Six years later, and I was still going "hmph, hmph, hmph" whenever I saw him. But on the outside, I stayed as still as stone. Like he had no effect on me whatsoever.

But the way they were acting, as if they didn't notice me, I didn't have a chance to do my aloof act.

"I'm telling you," Caroline said with just a hint of a Southern drawl, "you have grown two inches since I saw you." Then, she wrapped Angel inside her arms, as if Angel belonged to her.

"Mom, you saw me two weekends ago," Angel whined and laughed at the same time.

I squinted. There was that "Mom" again. And my eyes narrowed even more as the trio kissed and hugged as if they were a family.

"We have lots of gifts for you under the tree," Bobby said.

The greetings went on and on and on and I just stood there, shifting from one leg to the other. I swear I wanted to moonwalk right out of there. But I kept thinking about Angel...Angel...Angel.

"But before we do that, you have to say hello to everyone," Caroline said, taking Angel's hand. Then, leaning in closer, she added, "There are some very special people waiting to see you."

And still, I stood there, completely unnoticed. As Caroline led my daughter away, I could feel that green monster jealousy thing rising up inside of me. *This is my child,* I wanted to scream out.

Luckily, I didn't have a chance to do that because Angel had only taken a couple of steps away before she stopped. "Uh...Dad, Mom Caroline..." She turned around and ran back to me. "Mom's here, remember?"

Bobby shook his head slightly. "I'm so sorry." He took two giant steps back to where I was. "I get caught up with Angel every time." Then he gave me one of those Sunday hugs between church folks where there was two miles of space between us. "Merry Christmas, and thanks for coming."

"Merry Christmas, and thanks for having me." I squeezed the words through my lips.

Caroline didn't move from where she stood. "I'm sorry, I didn't even see you standing there. Merry Christmas," she said in a tone that didn't sound anything like she wanted me there. Then she held out her hand to Angel. "Come on, dear, your grandparents are waiting for you."

Angel looked up, and I nodded. "I'm right behind you."

With her long stride, Angel caught up to Caroline, but before Bobby and I could follow, the doorbell rang.

Without saying a word, he turned toward the front door, leaving me all by myself again. I looked to the left, then to the right, and decided to follow Angel and Caroline into the living room.

Now, I knew I was living a grand life, but standing here, I felt like I was living like a pauper. The living room hadn't been redecorated, and with the golden paint on the walls and all of the traditional furniture, you could tell that Caroline and Bobby were used to more than fine living. Their lives were all about elegant living.

"Mom, Dad," Caroline called out. "Look who's here."

A man and a woman turned, faced Caroline and Angel, and their smiles were immediate.

"Grandpa, Grandma," Angel exclaimed.

The way Angel called out to them made me raise my eyebrows. I could tell right off that these were Caroline's parents. I mean, one look at the woman—who was about five-seven, very toned and slender with silver hair that was pulled back in a bun—and you knew she was related to Caroline.

As Angel ran over to them and they hugged her, once again, I was left standing on the outside of the inner circle.

For a moment, I thought about going over to Caroline's parents and introducing myself. But I already felt like an intruder; there was no way I was gonna put myself out and end up feeling worse.

So, I just stayed on the side and watched Angel. It was so weird; this was the first time that I was seeing her in her other life. As they kept on hugging and kissing her, I wondered why Angel had never told me about Caroline's parents.

But then, how could I blame my daughter? It wasn't like I was warm and fuzzy whenever Angel talked about Caroline and Bobby. In fact, when she came home raving about this and that while she was with her father, I would just put on my headphones and turn the volume all the way up.

Now, I wished that I hadn't acted like that. I needed to be in every part of Angel's life. And it was going to start today. Right here. At this Christmas dinner.

I moved my eyes away from Angel for a moment, and then looked into the crowd that filled the living room. Without even knowing any of them, I could tell they were really sophisticated, far above my social grade. It was the way they stood and the way they chatted. Some of the men were smoking pipes—did people still do that?—and the women all sat with their ankles crossed and their backs straight as boards.

They sampled hors d'oeuvres and sipped champagne from the waiters who moved through the crowd almost unnoticed.

"Would you like something to drink?" a petite Asian woman asked me as she balanced the tray on one hand. "This is champagne," she said.

I leaned over. "Do you have any wine? Moscato?"

The woman smiled and nodded. "I'll bring you a glass," she whispered.

Good! Now, with a glass of Moscato, I'd be able to handle the rest of the evening. I stepped all the way into the living room into the mass of guests. This was still a bit overwhelming. I thought there were just going to be eight people here—the parents, Bobby and Caroline, and me and Angel.

But this...this was an event.

As I strolled through the gathering, I heard pieces of their worldly conversations about Syria and Russia, about the stock market and interest rates, about being bundlers for the next presidential election—if Hillary chose to run.

I shook my head. Didn't any of these people know that it was Christmas? I should've had Noon here with me. Me and my best friend would've shaken this crowd up. Yeah, we could've told them about Stevie and Joseline and Momma Dee. I giggled at that thought. Can you imagine the looks on these people's faces? Oh, yeah. A little *Love and Hip Hop* would really have taken the starch out of these stiff shirts.

"Here's your glass," the woman interrupted my thoughts. "Just let me know if you want another one."

"Thank you," I said, wanting to give the woman a kiss or at least a hug. I took that first sip and almost moaned out loud. After a second sip, I searched through the living room for Angel. But she was nowhere to be found. So, I took another sip, and kept walking through. I guess I was kinda searching for someone to look up, make eye contact, and invite me to join their crew. But as I eased by the people, I felt as if no one could see me. Like I was completely invisible. Of course, there were a few men who passed me a smile on the sly.

I sighed. From the time I was a kid 'til now, women didn't like me, and I knew it had a lot to do with my looks. And men...well, they only saw me for one thing, and I knew it had a lot to do with my looks. My looks: the story of my life.

But I wasn't even sure that I wanted anybody to ask me to join them. Because if they did, what would I say? I couldn't even be able to find Russia on a map—and I didn't care.

So I found a chair in the corner of the room, sat down, leaned back, crossed my legs, then sipped my wine until my glass was empty. I placed my glass on the floor, but it was only there for a moment. Another glass appeared, filled with my beloved Moscato. Clearly my wine supplier understood what it was like for me to be here.

A few more sips, and I became a connoisseur of the crowd. I figured out what each man did for a living, and I was convinced of why each of the women hated me.

But then, I wondered. I had been with Bobby for ten years, and he had never shared this world with me. Why not?

When we were together, our lives were filled with only two things: lots of partying with his Laker buddies and lots of sex at home. It was wonderful to me, but then again, I was nineteen, twenty, and twenty-one.

But what would have happened if Bobby had exposed me to more? What would've happened if when I were twenty-two, and twenty-three, and twenty-four, Bobby had taken me out to meet people like the ones who were here? Or if when I were twenty-five, twenty-six, and twenty-seven he would have taken me to the theatre, and the opera, and the ballet?

If he had done any of that, would I have matured into a woman that he would've wanted to really call his own? If he had done all of that, would he have still dumped me when I was twenty-eight? Or would he have still chosen Caroline because not only was she already refined, but she was a woman who had her own means?

I shook her head. Bobby and I were old news, so why was I wasting any time even thinking about him? I needed to get away from these funky thoughts quick!

I stood up, but then, I stood still. Where was I going to go? I hadn't seen Angel in a while. And even Bobby and Caroline were nowhere in sight.

Strolling over to the fireplace, I studied the gold frames on the mantel. These pictures told the story of the Johnsons. Pictures of Bobby and Caroline, all hugged up and happy. And then there were pictures of Bobby, Caroline, *and* Angel.

I picked up the photo on the end. The three were on a beach, holding each other and smiling like this was the best time of their lives. I had to put that one down. But then, I made another mistake and picked up another picture. This one was with Caroline and Angel, both in sapphire gowns. And Bobby stood in the middle in a tuxedo.

This was my child, but they had claimed Angel as theirs. It was like Caroline had stolen my life!

I put the photo back in place, then glanced around at the room, the furniture, the people. This should have all been mine, and it would've been if Bobby had nurtured me and then made the right choice.

"Would you like another glass?"

My Asian friend was back, and it wasn't until she asked the question that I even realized my glass was once again empty.

But just a few moments after I said, "Yes," I had a new glass in my hand. This time, though, the wine didn't make me feel as good as before. No matter how fast I drank it.

I strolled back over to my chair, plopped down a little harder than I'd planned to, and as Nat King Cole crooned about chestnuts roasting, I took quite a few more sips of my wine.

And then, I don't know why it happened, but tears started streaming down my face. I put down my glass and held my head in my hands.

This was a miserable Christmas, and what was worse was that I had no place else to go.

Thirteen

"Mom!" Angel tried to whisper. "What's wrong?"

I lifted my head and had to blink a couple of times to bring my daughter into focus. "What?"

"You're crying. What's wrong?"

"I'm not crying," I said as I wiped my eyes. "It's just that...I couldn't find you...and I was sitting here alone," I sobbed.

"Mom," Angel looked over her shoulder to see if anyone was watching us.

But all around us, the Christmas celebration continued with music and laughter. Just like for the hour that I'd been here, no one seemed to notice me.

Angel slid onto the arm of the chair and put her arm around me. "I'm sorry you were by yourself, but I was with Mom and Dad..."

"She's not your mother," I snapped.

"You know what I mean. I've just been walking through the party because there were people they wanted me to meet."

"Well," I wiped away my tears with the back of my hand, "while you were walking around, I've been by myself."

"I'm sorry."

"I don't have anybody to talk to."

"You can talk to anybody."

"I don't fit in here. I know it and everybody here knows it, too."

"If you talk to them, I'm sure they'll talk back to you. Remember what you used to tell me? You have to be friendly to make friends."

I couldn't believe that she was throwing back stuff at me. Yeah, I was right to tell her that, but that was when she was in kindergarten! This was different.

I guess it was my silence that made Angel say, "I won't leave you anymore."

I hated that I was whiny and clingy. What I wanted to do was tell Angel to just go off with her father and stepmother. I'd be fine. After all, I was a grown woman; I could certainly sit in a room by myself.

But being here around these people...I didn't feel grown. Really, at this moment, Angel probably felt more grown than I did.

So after Angel told me that she wouldn't leave me, all I could say was, "Thanks."

And right at that moment, Caroline hurried into the room and zeroed in on Angel.

"Sweetheart, come here," she motioned with her hand. "The Petersons, the couple we were telling you about from New York, just arrived. I want you to meet them."

Angel nodded, stood, and took my hand. "Come on," she whispered.

I shook my head. "I don't think Caroline wants to introduce me to anybody."

"Of course she does," Angel said. "And anyway, anybody who wants to meet me should get to meet my fabulous mom."

For the first time since I got here, I smiled. "You're such a good daughter." Then I stood up, and wobbled a bit. "Whoa." I had to hold onto Angel to steady myself.

"Mom," Angel whispered, "are you drunk?"

"Drunk? No. I'd have to drink to get drunk, and I've only had a couple of glasses of wine. I just stood up too fast. Felt a little dizzy, but I'm good now."

"Okay," Angel said, though she gripped my hand a little tighter.

As Angel walked, I did my best to keep up with her. It was already hard enough because she had such a long stride. But now, I was unsteady on my feet. How many glasses of wine had I finished off?

Angel zigzagged through the guests (making me even more dizzy) as she made her way from the living room, through the foyer, to the other side of the house, where Caroline stood at the door of the library, chatting with a man and a woman.

"Mom," Angel called out to Caroline and I could feel it...my blood pressure was rising.

With a smile, Caroline turned, but then she frowned when she looked at me. The smile was still in her voice, though, when Caroline said, "Come here, sweetheart, I want you to meet Mr. and Mrs. Peterson." Turning to the couple, Caroline said, "This is our daughter, Angel."

"It is wonderful to meet you," the man with snow-white hair that almost matched his skin said. "You are as beautiful as your mother said."

Caroline put her arms around Angel's shoulders and beamed.

"Yes," the woman standing next to the man piped in, "you're simply lovely."

"Uh..." I grunted.

"Oh, I'm sorry," Angel said. She smiled as she began, "This is..."

Before she could finish, Caroline cut Angel off, "Oh, yes, this is Asia."

"Nice to meet you, Asia," the man and the woman said together.

I frowned. That's it? That's how she was going to introduce me? She was dismissing me like I wasn't an important part of this relationship.

"So, young lady," Mr. Peterson said to Angel, "we have a lot to talk about."

"Excuse me," I jumped in. My voice came out a little louder than I expected. "My name is Asia, Angel's mother."

The man glanced at Caroline, then turned back to me with a look that told me he didn't have any idea what I was talking about.

So, I made it clear to him. "I'm Asia, Angel's mother," I said, using my thumb to point to my chest the whole time.

"We know that," Caroline said, though her lips hardly moved. Then she had the nerve to turn her back on me. And I'm telling you, I was about to go all the way off.

My daughter knew me well, though. She could feel it; she knew it was about to be on. "Mom," she whispered. "Mom, please."

"Please what?" I asked; this time I didn't even try to keep my voice down.

Angel took my hand and pulled me away.

"Where are we going?" I grumbled. I wanted to jerk my arm away from the hold she had on me. I wanted to curse Caroline out and then just go home.

But instead, I followed my daughter as she dragged me through the long hallway and back into the kitchen where chefs and waitstaff moved about, putting the final touches on the dinner. Together, we weaved through the space until we were on the other side, standing in the breakfast nook.

While the staff rushed around us, Angel whispered, "Mom, what are you doing?"

"What're you talking about?"

"I'm talking about out there," Angel said, pointing toward the front of the house. "You were acting all mad and talking loud."

"You need to talk to your evil stepmother. What was Broom Hilda trying to do, huh? Introducing you as her daughter."

"Mom, she always does that."

"Then she needs to stop it." I leaned in closer. "She is not your mother."

Angel backed up, frowning. I guess she could smell the wine on my breath. "I know she's not my mother," she said. "Everybody knows that she's not my mother. She just doesn't like to use the word 'step.' And neither do I, 'cause Mom Caroline has always been nice to me."

"Well, she isn't being nice to me. She invited me over here just to make me feel like a fool."

"No, she didn't! She's just busy because there are so many people here, and she has to make sure that everything is right. If she wasn't so busy, she would talk to you more. She really wants you here, but Mom, you've got to act right."

"Act right?" I felt my shoulders hunch up and I crossed my arms. "Who are you talking to that way? I'm not even doing anything. In fact, you know what? Let me just get the hell out of here."

"No! Mom, please!" She paused, she blinked, she swallowed as if she were trying to hold back tears and sobs. "I just want everybody to get along, and I really want you here with me. *It's Christmas.*"

It took less than two seconds for me to sober up and soften up. "Oh, baby, I'm not going anywhere. Don't cry. I'll try to," I paused and forced the next words out, "act right."

Angel stepped back. "Will you?" she asked, sounding like she wanted to do some kind of pinky promise with me.

I nodded, then looked around. "All I need is another glass of wine."

Angel shook her head hard. "I don't think that's gonna help."

"Yeah, it will. I need it so that I can loosen up and get rid of all this stuff I'm feeling."

"Angel!"

We both turned at the sound of Caroline's voice, and I stared her down as she moved to where we were standing. Her gaze moved from Angel to me, then back to Angel. "What are you doing in here?"

"Nothing. I was just showing my mom the kitchen."

"Oh," Caroline said. Her eyes narrowed as she studied Angel. "Well, your father is looking for you. Daphne and her parents just arrived."

"Cool!" Angel turned to me. "Mom, you have got to meet my best friend, Daphne. Well, she's my best friend when I stay here, but you're gonna love her."

"Okay." I was glad to get away from Caroline because if I stayed with her for one moment, I didn't know what I'd do.

But just as I took a couple of steps, Caroline called my name.

When I turned around, she asked, "Can I talk to you?"

I moved back to her, and Angel did, too. "What do you want?" I wondered if she could hear it in my tone—that if she wanted a fight, she'd chosen the wrong one.

"Mom!" Angel called out, but to be honest, I wasn't sure which mom she was talking to.

Then together, Caroline and I said, "It's all right."

Still, my daughter didn't move.

"Go ahead," I told her, a little more forcefully. But I said it with such a wide smile, that Angel relaxed a little. "We'll be fine here," I added. "We're just gonna have a little talk."

Caroline gave Angel her own nod of assurance.

"Okay," Angel said softly. She began moving, walking backwards so that she could keep her eyes on us. Without saying a word, she pleaded with both of us, and with our smiles, we made promises to her.

But once Angel was out of our sight, it was on. All smiles were gone and there was no promise that I planned to keep.

"What was that out there?" Caroline asked, getting right to her point.

"That's what I should be asking you. It felt like you were trying to push me to the side, like I didn't matter."

At first, Caroline didn't speak, as if she were letting my words hang in the air. As if she were telling me those were my words, not hers, but...

Then she said, "This is our home, these are our friends, and I would appreciate it if you would take that into consideration the next time you open your mouth."

"Then stop trying to belittle me and embarrass me."

"What are you talking about? I was simply introducing Angel to the Petersons."

"Introducing her as if you were her mother. And that's what you need to understand." I got in Caroline's face. "Nothing will ever make you Angel's mother. She's my daughter, and you need to respect that; you need to respect me."

"Oh, the way you respected me when you slept with my husband? For all of those years?"

I pulled back a little. Was that what this was about? I gave her a half-chuckle. "Really, Caroline? You're still holding onto that?"

"Holding onto it? As if that were something small." Now she got in my face. "You slept with my husband, Asia. And I will never forgive you for that."

I have to admit, the venom in her voice made me back up a little. "So then, why did you invite me here?"

She didn't hesitate for a moment. "To remind you, Asia. To remind you of your place."

I frowned. My place?

Then, she broke it down for me. "I wanted you to see Bobby's life," she said with a smirk. "And to see that you would never fit in here."

Okay, this chick was bunny-rabbit-boiling crazy. "So you're saying that you still see me as a threat?" I laughed. "This is classic. Sweetie, I don't want your husband." I paused. "Though all this proves is that I could have him any time I wanted him."

Now, the truth was, I didn't believe that. From the moment Bobby had told me that our affair was over, he didn't even come close to giving me any signs that he still wanted me. But for some reason, this heffa wasn't so sure about her husband.

And I'd just scored a point, because the way her eyes darkened let me know that she *was* worried about Bobby. What was going on in their lives?

"All I want to do," Caroline began in that high-brow tone of hers, "is find a way to keep the peace for the rest of this evening."

"Okay, I'm down for that," I said with my arms still crossed. "We'll make it through tonight, and then you won't ever have to worry about me coming back."

She smiled as if I'd just made her very happy. "Well, in a few years, we won't have to worry about any contact. We only have a couple of years of co-parenting."

"You mean, Bobby and I only have a few more years," I corrected her.

Caroline smirked, "If that's the way you see it, then yes."

"And it's more than a few years. But you're right, once Angel graduates from high school, there won't be any reason for any of us to see each other."

Now Caroline's smile got so wide, I had to frown. "What?"

She turned her back on me...again, and started to walk away, but I caught her by her arm. Caroline looked down to where I held her, then her eyes slowly rose.

I released my grip, but not because I was afraid of her. I just wanted to know what had her grinnin' like that. "What? What did I say that you find so funny?"

Caroline pushed her shoulders back. "Okay, you want to know, Asia? We'll be out of your life sooner than you think."

When she didn't say anything more, I said, "Stop talking in circles. Just say what you have to say."

"All right. You and I won't have to see each other once Angel *enters* high school. Because she'll be going to school in New York. We're moving there...me, Bobby, and Angel."

"What?" I couldn't stop my eyes from blinking. All I was trying to do was understand her words.

"Yes, Angel will be able to pursue her modeling career and attend Performing Arts High School. And then, all of this stuff that goes on between us will be minimized. You won't have to deal with me, and I won't have to deal with you." It sounded like her last words gave her great pleasure.

"What are you talking about? Angel's not going to New York. She's not going anywhere with you."

This time when Caroline turned away, she didn't stop moving.

"I'm her mother!" I yelled out. "No matter what you try to do, I'm her mother!"

But Caroline never turned back, and seconds later, she was gone.

I just stood there, with all the clanging of pots and pans, dishes and glasses. But even though I heard all of that, Caroline's words, still ringing in my ears, were louder. What was she talking about? New York?

I thought about those people out there, the Petersons. They were from New York. Did they have anything to do with what Caroline was talking about?

But she and Bobby couldn't take Angel to New York. We shared custody; the court would never allow it. He couldn't just up and take her.

Then I thought about who Bobby was, the beloved ex-Laker who was now a real estate developer. He could probably pay off a judge.

Even if he did that, though, Angel wouldn't leave me...would she? In that moment, I thought of all of my daughter's dreams. How she wanted to model, and act, and dance, and sing. She didn't have to go to New York, though, to make that happen...did she?

Oh, god! I didn't know what this was about, but I didn't feel good. I was too weak to stand, so I just fell back onto the bench. As one of the waiters passed, I grabbed a glass from the tray, and in one gulp, I swallowed half the bubbly liquid and closed my eyes as it burned all the way down my throat.

But the champagne didn't make it any better. I hated to admit it, but I could feel the fear boiling inside of me. It wasn't just fear alone. It was fear and truth.

And the truth was if Bobby wanted it, there might not be any way that I could stop him from taking Angel from me. Things like this were happening all the time. I saw it a lot on that TV show *Snapped.* That's why a lot of those women snapped!

Oh, god! I was gonna lose my little girl, and then what would I do?

Fourteen

"Miss! Miss!"

They were calling out to me as I sauntered down the runway, crisscrossing one of my long legs in front of the other. I got to the end of the long stage, pivoted, and then saw—it wasn't my face.

Angel was the one who was strutting her stuff. Angel was the one they were calling and photographing. Angel was the model.

"Miss! Miss!"

And then, the earth moved. At least it felt like the earth at first, but it was mostly just my arm. I tried to pull my eyelids apart, but it felt like they were stuck together with Krazy Glue. With a moan and another push, I finally got my eyes opened.

"Miss! Ms. Johnson is serving dinner."

"What?" I said, looking up and into the face of an Asian woman who looked so familiar to me.

"Dinner," the woman said. "They're ready for everyone to take their seats in the tent out back, Miss."

Dinner? It took me a minute to even figure out where I was. It was Christmas...with Angel, Bobby...and Caroline.

As I sat up straight, I moaned. My butt hurt, and that's when I remembered where I was. Still in the kitchen. Sitting on this hard bench in the corner. And all around me, the staff rushed by, moving even faster now as if something big were about to happen.

What was I still doing in here? I closed my eyes and tried to remember. There was that exchange with Caroline and then the passing waiter who'd given me a glass of champagne. Right after that, I'd spotted my Asian friend, and she'd refilled my glass with the Moscato that I'd really wanted. Yes, she was the one who'd just woken me up.

But after that? Did I have another glass?

A flash of a memory hit me. No, I didn't have another glass; I'd asked my friend for the whole bottle! And there it was—the empty bottle of Moscato sitting in the middle of the table.

I pressed the tips of my fingers against my temples, trying to soften the throb. But the way my head ached was the least of my worries. If Angel saw me now, she would have no questions. She wouldn't have to ask—I was officially drunk.

I had to find my daughter, though, but when I stood up, it was only because I was holding onto the edge of the table that I didn't fall down. It took a few moments, but finally the world steadied, and I was able to step slowly through the kitchen into the hallway where a whole bunch of people walked by, moving toward the back of the house.

The walk from the kitchen to the hall had been long enough; I didn't have the energy to go staggering through the house looking for Angel. She'd just have to catch up with me in the backyard.

At the sliding glass doors, several men and women stood in matching tuxedos with clipboards in their hands.

"What's your name?" one of the women asked me.

"Uh...Asia Ingrum."

The woman scanned through the sheets she held. "You're at table sixteen."

If I'd had enough energy, I would've rolled my eyes. Really? Did it take all of this for a Christmas dinner?

I stepped onto the parquet platform that covered the grass and entered the humongous tent. I paused for a moment, taking in the Winter Wonderland that Bobby and Caroline had created: from the mini Christmas trees with glittering lights that stood in the corners of the tent, to the angels that floated above, it felt like Christmas in heaven.

At any other time, in any other place, I would've looked around and probably really liked this set up. But right now, all I wanted to do was find my table and sit down.

Of course, table sixteen was all the way on the other side of the room, and I had to stumble through the maze to get there. All of the noise—talking and laughing and music—was making my headache worse.

It felt like it took two forevers to get to that table, and when I slid down into that chair, I had to resist putting my head down, too. I really wanted to do that, but it would be too embarrassing for Angel if she came in here and found me that way.

All I had to do was suck it up for the next hour or two, and then I could go back to the wonderful world that was my home.

Then after I slept, I'd grill Angel on this New York mess Caroline told me about. Though to be honest, I was beginning to think that Caroline had made it all up. Yeah, it was a lie just to make me feel bad. And really, it had worked.

"Mom!"

Even with the way my head ached, I smiled as I spotted Angel bouncing across the room with two other girls behind her. My daughter glowed with happiness, and right then, I forgot about the rest of the day. Yeah, I'd been pretty miserable, wanting to get out of here a thousand times. But looking at Angel's face right now—this was what it was all about. Her joy, her Christmas. Anything for my daughter.

"Mom! I've been looking for you," Angel squealed.

"Well, you've found me," I said, glad that my daughter hadn't seen me just minutes before passed out in the kitchen.

Angel turned to her friends, "This is my mom. Mom, this is Daphne and Megan."

"Hi, Mrs. Johnson," the two girls said together.

"Oh, her name is not Mrs. Johnson." I looked up and wondered when Caroline had swooped down on her broom. "Her name is *Ingrum*," Caroline said as if that were a bad thing. Before I could curse her out, Caroline said, "Now, Angel, you won't be sitting here. You'll be sitting with me and your dad. Your friends are at this table."

"Mom, I want to sit with Daphne and Megan."

Sit with Daphne and Megan? I wanted to ask my daughter what about sitting with me—her mother. But my thoughts didn't stay long on that question because I was trying to figure out what Caroline had said. It didn't take me long. Especially when Daphne and Megan sat down. And then, two other girls joined us.

That was when I got it for sure.

I jumped up so fast, I knocked my chair over. I didn't bother to pick it up; my focus was on Caroline. As I stomped toward the table where Caroline was sitting with my child, every moment of this day replayed in my head, and I was so mad that it felt like I was on fire. By the time I got to the table, my fury had to be showing.

Leaning across the table, I put my finger in Caroline's face. "If it wasn't Christmas, I'd call you a son-of-a..."

"Mom!" Angel exclaimed, leaping from her chair.

"Asia!" Caroline's eyes were wide with innocence, though she knew what was up. I could see it in the way she was fighting to hold her laughter inside. "What's wrong with you?" she asked me.

"What's wrong? You know what's wrong, heffa!" I shouted. "You sat me at the kiddie table. I should be sitting up here with you...and my daughter."

"First of all, this table is for family—"

"Caroline!" Bobby yelled out as if he knew that wasn't the right thing to say to me.

But his wife ignored him. Caroline continued, "And secondly, I didn't sit you at the children's table. I sat you at the only open table. If you remember, you didn't tell us until yesterday that you were coming, and the seating plan was already completed."

"Well, you should've done it over, you trick!"

As gasps filled the room, Bobby grabbed ahold of me. "You don't want to do this," he whispered in my ear.

But I snatched my arm from his grasp. "You knew exactly what you were doing," I shouted. "You've been trying to embarrass me, trying to put me in my place ever since I got here. If it wasn't Christmas, I'd beat your—"

"Mom!" Angel grabbed my hand, but just like I did to Bobby, I jerked away from her. "No, you sit down and stay out of this, Angel. I need to tell this skank about herself."

"Mom," Angel cried, as she looked around at all the wide eyes that were on us. "You're embarrassing me."

It was the tears that had started rolling down Angel's cheeks that made me pause, back up, and wobble away to my table.

I grabbed my purse, stepped over the fallen chair, and marched out of the room with as much dignity as my unsteady legs allowed. I should've done this a long time ago. Yeah, I was trying to stay for Angel, and I didn't want to spend Christmas at home, alone. But anything was going to be better than this.

"Mom!" I heard Angel crying behind me, but I couldn't stop.

That made me feel bad because I always wanted to comfort my daughter. But how could I comfort her when I needed someone to comfort me?

I could feel everyone staring at me, but do you think I cared? Not one of these bourgie snobs had said a single word to me today. So I didn't give a flying frig what they had to say now!

As I staggered from the backyard and into the house, I could still hear the cries of Angel. She didn't catch me, though. Not until I was almost at the front door.

"Mom, where are you going?"

"Home!"

"You can't," Angel said with tears crawling down her cheeks.

"You think I'm going to stay here?" I asked Angel. "Caroline doesn't want me here, and I can't believe that I let you and your father talk me into this. I'm going home!" I tried to take a few more steps. That's all I needed to get to the front door, but my world was swaying again.

"Mom, you can't drive."

I leaned against the wall. Angel had a point. But still, I had to get out of here.

"Okay, maybe this isn't the best time for me to be driving. I'll call a cab."

"Even if you can get a cab today, your car will still be here. How are you gonna get it home?"

I shook her head. It was a good thing that Angel was doing all the thinking right now.

"You can go up to my room," Angel said. "You can rest, and I'll stay there with you."

Rest! Oh, my god. That word sounded so wonderful. All I wanted to do was close my eyes, even for just a few minutes. That would be the best Christmas gift right now.

So when Angel took my hand and led me up the steps, I didn't protest at all. We had to move slowly, though; the winding staircase made me swoon. At the top, I felt like I was walking the longest mile, following Angel down the hallway. But finally, we stopped.

It wasn't until I stepped inside that I realized this was the first time I'd been in Angel's bedroom at Bobby's house. As I took in the surroundings, I wondered why Angel ever wanted to come home.

This wasn't a bedroom, it was a two-room suite, filled with all the pleasures of a teenage heaven. From the sixty-inch television that was mounted to the wall in the sitting area, to the surround-sound speakers in the corners, and the canopy bed that floated in the middle of the humongous bedroom.

And that's where my eyes settled—right on that bed. Moving as fast as I could, I got to that bed, then dropped down, sinking into the coverings. Either this duvet was the softest duvet on earth, or I was truly drunk because this felt like I was floating on a cloud.

Right away, I closed my eyes, but then I felt the bed sink just a little. When I opened my eyes, Angel was lying next to me, staring into my face.

It took a lot of effort, but I pushed myself up and shook my head. "No, baby, you go on back downstairs."

"But I don't want to leave you alone."

"It's okay."

"I don't want you to leave."

That pissed me off, but I wasn't mad at her. I was mad at myself. On Christmas, the only thing I'd given my daughter was the burden of taking care of me. "I promise you, Angel, I won't leave. I promise. Go on down, enjoy the rest of your dinner, and when everyone leaves, I'll be here waiting for you."

Angel nodded and blinked back tears. "I'm sorry, Mom. I'm sorry that this is such a horrible Christmas."

"No, baby. Don't you be sorry. I'm sorry that I didn't handle it better. But, I'm going to be fine now. So you go on back down there, and don't worry about me."

Angel kissed my cheek, then ambled out of the room like the events of the day weighed heavy on her body and her mind.

I waited until I was sure that Angel was gone before I lowered my head once again. There were at least one hundred people in their backyard, but in that room, it was as silent as the middle of the night.

I hugged one of the pillows and wished that I could start this day all over. Maybe begin the week again when I'd first received the call from Bobby. I would have surely said no to this horrible idea.

The light tap on the door made me raise my head. I was sure it was just Angel coming back, but then Bobby peeked his head inside.

"Just checking on you," he said as he entered the room.

Moving slowly, I flung my legs over the side of the bed and sat up, ready for this fight. "I know you're upset with me, but..."

He held up his hands. "No, I'm not. I'm just sorry about all of this. I thought this would work out; I thought it would be fine."

I blew out an exhausted breath. "I tried. Even with everything that Caroline was doing to me, I tried. But when she told me that the two of you were taking Angel away from me..." The rest of the words caught in my throat.

"What?" Bobby lowered himself to the bed.

"She said you were taking Angel to New York and then she wouldn't have to deal with me anymore."

"Asia...I'm sorry," he said softly. "She shouldn't have said that."

"How can you do this to me, Bobby?"

He shook his head, and I was surprised when he took my hands in his. "We're not going to do anything. We were just talking about it; nothing's final."

I looked down and stared at where he held me. "I don't know what I would do without my Angel." My voice trembled. "I wouldn't make it." When I glanced up, my tears dripped onto our hands. "Please, don't take her from me, Bobby. She's all I have."

With his thumb, he wiped my tears, first from my right cheek, then my left. I don't know why, but the way he touched me, so gently, made me cry more. That was when he pulled me close to him and wrapped his arms around me. I closed my eyes and rested my head and my burdens on his shoulders.

"I promise you, Asia, you're going to be fine," he whispered into my ear.

I leaned back and asked, "How can you say that? If Angel goes away, I won't be fine."

"I'll make sure that you are," he said. "I promise." And then, there was this moment and this thing that passed between us. And after another moment, Bobby leaned forward. Then, with the same gentleness that he'd just used with his hands, he pressed his lips against mine. I closed my eyes and received him. And I marveled at how he felt exactly the same as six years ago. So, so good!

When I leaned back, I thought he was going to jump up. Say that I tricked him or something. But he didn't do any of that. He just took my hands back into his. "Feel better?"

That was when I saw the shadow at the door. I didn't even have to turn my head; I saw her without hardly moving...Caroline. She stood at the doorway, with her hands folded, her lips pursed, and her eyes narrowed. Nothing moved— except for her nose. Even from all those feet away, I could see Caroline's nostrils flaring.

I turned my eyes back to Bobby. "Yes, I do feel better. Thank you." And in case Caroline had missed it, I leaned forward, and this time, I pulled Bobby into my arms. I closed my eyes and hugged him the way I used to.

When I pulled back a little and glanced toward the door, she was gone. That was when I let Bobby go. I said, "There're a lot of people waiting for you downstairs."

He nodded. "Yeah, and Caroline is going to wonder where I am."

I said nothing.

"Are you going to be all right up here?"

I nodded. "I really just want to lie down for a while. Get myself together."

"Do that." He kissed my forehead, then stood.

I sat in place as I watched him walk toward the door. When he got there, he paused, turned around, and then gave me a smile that felt as good as his kiss.

When he stepped into the hallway, I lay down, but this time, I didn't close my eyes. Instead I thought about that kiss, our kiss, and his smile. And I wondered what was all of that. And then I wondered if there would be more. 'Cause I definitely wanted more.

For the first time since I'd gotten that call from Bobby asking about this dinner, I really smiled. Christmas had always been my favorite holiday, but what a disaster this day had been.

But while the day had been crap, tonight was a different story.

I pressed my fingers against my lips feeling like Bobby's were still there. Yeah, tonight had been some night. Some holy night!

Forever an Ex

Pastor Beverly Ford

Fifteen

The sanctuary was silent when I stepped inside.

Which is exactly what I would expect on a Friday. But on this day, two days after Christmas, it was silent, though it was not empty.

I stood at the door that led from the sanctuary to my administrative offices, taking in the women that I'd called to be here.

First, there was Sheridan, sitting on the front pew, right in the center. Exactly where I would expect her to be. Her head was bowed, and her forehead rested on her clasped hands. There was no doubt; she was in prayer.

About eight rows back from Sheridan was Kendall, sitting on the left in the last seat. And she was on the edge of the pew, as if she were ready to make a run for it at the first sign of trouble. Inside, I chuckled. At least she wasn't in the back row, which is where Kendall usually sat, where she'd been sitting for the last six years whenever she *did* come to church.

And finally, there was my niece. I sighed as I watched Asia, texting on her phone, then checking her watch, then going back to texting. She paced in the aisle behind the last row. As if she were so busy and didn't have time for this.

Yeah, right! My niece and her life? She didn't have anywhere else to be.

I moved silently across the carpet, and it wasn't until my voice echoed through the large space when I said, "Good morning," that the three lifted their heads.

Gesturing with my hand, I motioned for Kendall and Asia to join me up front. Asia walked toward me first, and then she paused when she got to Kendall's row. As if she needed Kendall with her to make the last part of the journey. Then the two of them walked shoulder-to-shoulder, moving slowly as if they were taking that long walk down death row.

With solemn faces, they gazed at me, looking like this was the last place they wanted to be, and I was the last person they wanted to see. I had to fight hard to hold back a smile. I knew my niece was the drama queen. But Kendall? I guess that's what a six-year friendship would do.

Though I have to admit, friendship was the last thing that I'd expected to come out of the circle of women I'd put together. When I'd introduced them, my hope was the women, who were all going through situations with their exes, would support each other and pray together. And I'd hope that a side effect would be that the older women would influence my niece in a positive way.

I'd been right. The group that I called The Ex Files, had turned out to be more than just a support group and a prayer group. It had been the impetus for their friendship.

But after the calls I'd received yesterday, it seemed that, while the friendships were intact, the ladies hadn't moved as far away from their exes as I'd hoped. Maybe they were still supporting each other, but it seemed like they were supporting each other in their dysfunction. All these years later, and they still had major issues with those same men.

I leaned against the railing in front of the altar, crossed my arms, and waited for Kendall and Asia to take seats next to Sheridan. Then I let them sit in silence of the sanctuary for a moment before I said, "Thank you all for coming."

"As if we had a choice," my niece mumbled.

I was used to Asia's smart remarks. And usually, I would go in on her. But I kept my focus on my purpose, this meeting.

"Let me get right to the point of why I called you here." I paused and looked at Asia. "Calling you here and not giving you a choice."

My niece tucked her chin to her chest.

"I understand the three of you had very interesting Christmases."

I hadn't told any of them why I had called them to the church; I hadn't even told them that the others would be here. So I'm sure my words were a surprise. But not one of the ladies said a word. Instead, they all looked away as if it were too difficult now to make eye contact with me.

"We need to talk about this," I said. "Or rather, I need to talk, and you need to listen.

"When I first came up with The Ex Files, I wanted to bring women who were in similar circumstances together so that you could talk together, cry together, pray together. And I thank God that over the years, you've really bonded. But what Christmas has shown me is that while you have moved forward in certain parts of your lives, the three of you are still stuck in some way with your exes. And since these men will be in your lives, since they will all forever be an ex, you have to find a way to deal with these situations."

I paused, so that their spirits could digest my words.

My eyes moved to Sheridan first. Though her head was up and her eyes were on me, I had the feeling that she was still praying inside. That's just how Sheridan was; she was a prayerful woman who understood the need to take her cares to The Lord. That's why I was so surprised to find out that she was still in bondage over what happened between her and Quentin.

I walked over, then knelt in front of her. "Your mother called me," I said.

"She did?"

I nodded. "I heard all about your lunch with Quentin and his fiancée."

Both Kendall and Asia gasped, and that surprised me a little. I would've thought the three of them would've talked by now. But I guess all of their Christmases were traumatic, and they needed time to process it before they could share it.

I held Sheridan's hands within mine. "I want you to get this and get this good...you are not the reason that Quentin is gay." I paused so that those words could sink in. "You are not his sin, Sheridan. But you've got to know that you are not his savior either."

"Whoa," Kendall and Asia said together.

My words made an impact on Kendall and Asia, but at first, I wasn't sure about Sheridan. She stayed quiet, holding my hands, not moving at all. And then, tears welled in her eyes.

I wasn't trying to make her cry, but I really needed her to understand this. "Nothing with Quentin happened because of you. And where Quentin goes from here...that's not on you either." Again I paused before I asked, "Do you get that?"

When Sheridan nodded, a tear dropped from her eye. I wasn't sure if she got it totally, but she understood what I was saying and that was the beginning.

I pushed myself up and, in that moment, was so glad that I worked hard to stay in shape. But when I stood in front of Kendall, I decided not to crouch down again. This time, I sat on the pew.

Turning my body to the side, I now held Kendall's hands. "My dear Kendall. Your dad called me, and I'm so sorry."

I waited for Kendall to say something, but her face remained as hard as I knew her heart was. Kendall, the strong one. The one who didn't care, the one who hardly cried. The one who had been wounded the most.

"I'm going to be here for you and your dad. In fact, I'm going over to his house to pray with him this afternoon."

"Thank you, Pastor," she whispered.

"But listen to me," I began, "as your father is fighting a cancer, you have one within you that is eating you up inside. You have a cancer that is trying to destroy you just like your father's is trying to destroy him." I waited, hoping that Kendall would speak. But when she said nothing, I told her what she already knew. "My dear, you're going to have to find a way to deal with your unforgiveness."

She shrugged as if everything that I'd just said was no big deal. "If you're talking about Sabrina and Anthony, I don't have any issues anymore, Pastor."

"You don't?"

She shook her head. "Nope."

"Okay," I said. "Do this for me; look up at that altar. Look at that cross and tell me that you have forgiven Sabrina and Anthony."

Kendall raised her eyes, but then looked down right away. She didn't say anything.

Exactly! She could lie to me, she could even lie to herself, but she could never lie to God. I squeezed her hands. "What you went through with Sabrina and Anthony...I can't even imagine. I know you've said in the past that Sabrina and Anthony are a better match than you were with him..."

"Yeah, they are." Her tone still remained nonchalant. But there was just a little quiver in a voice. A little quiver that let me know that the hard shield around her heart was breaking away.

I said, "Still, the way it went down, what happened between them—it may have ended up right, but when it began, it was wrong." She squeezed my hands a little, though I think it was just a reflex. Inside, she was just agreeing with me. I kept on, "But here's the thing, Kendall, the entire Christian doctrine, all that we believe, all that we love...is about forgiveness. God's forgiveness.

"And God demands that we give to others exactly what He's given to us. He demands that we forgive. But it's not for the other person. He demands it so that unforgiveness doesn't grow like a cancer within us."

She pressed her eyelids together as if she were doing everything in her power to hold back her emotions.

I said, "God truly wants us to get this forgiveness thing. Because if you don't forgive people, God can never forgive you. And that's not me saying that; that's scriptural. I know you know that."

She nodded, but I was never sure when it came to Kendall. She was the one I could never read.

But there was not too much more that I could say. So, I left her with, "I want you to go home and read Matthew 6:14–15. I want you to read it. I want you to study it. I want you to write it out on index cards and post it all around your house. I want you to pray for more than understanding. I want you to pray that you will get the understanding all the way down to your soul so that the understanding will lead to a change in your heart."

Kendall nodded, but again, I just wasn't sure. All I could do from this point was what I'd always been doing. All I could do was pray for her.

With a sigh, I sat on the other side of Asia. My beautiful niece who didn't know just how beautiful she really was. Asia had never been able to understand that she was more than her physical being. She thought that her looks, her body, were all that she had to offer a man. She thought that her looks, her body, were what was going to find her true love.

Oh, for this child to understand that loving God first and herself second was all that she needed. But in all the years that I'd loved this girl, I'd never been able to convince her. This message couldn't come from the outside; this was something that Asia was going to have to search for inside, and God would reveal it to her.

I tried my best not to worry about anything in life; truly, I took everything to The Lord. But I had to work extra hard on doing that with Asia because it was difficult not to worry since she was in her mid-thirties now. So when was she going to learn this lesson? My fear was that she would eventually learn it, but that the lesson would come with a great fall.

I pushed her hair over her shoulder and smiled. "My dear, dear Asia. Do you know how much I love you?"

"I know that, Aunt Beverly. I love you, too."

"I just wish you loved yourself as much."

She rolled her eyes, and I knew what that was about. She'd heard this from me before, and I didn't care what kind of an attitude she got; she was about to hear it again. I would say it, shout it, scream it until she got it.

When Angel called me and told me what happened at their Christmas dinner, I was not surprised. In fact, it was what I expected. Caroline Johnson had been hurt by my niece, and hurt people, hurt people. Caroline needed counseling and prayer as much as Asia. But while I could pray for Caroline, my concern was my niece.

"I know what you're up to," I said.

Asia turned toward me with a frown.

"It's in my spirit," I said. "I know what you're up to with Bobby."

It was the way Asia hesitated for just a millisecond before she said, "I'm not up to anything," that let me know that I was right. Not that I had any doubts. What I told Asia was the truth. God had dropped the truth into my spirit.

"You're trying to fool everyone, Asia. Probably even trying to fool yourself. But this is what I know...do not be deceived: God is not mocked, for whatever one sows, that will he also reap," I said. Now while I always spoke the Word of God, I didn't usually go around quoting scriptures. That was just too heavenly for me. But I felt like Asia didn't need to hear any interpretation. She needed to hear the exact words from God.

Then my niece shocked me. She nodded. "That's in Galatians."

I'm sure my eyebrows shot all the way up to the top of my head. I'm not one to judge anyone's relationship with God, but I have to say, Asia just made me want to shut my mouth! Sure, she was in church every Sunday, but I thought that was just because she didn't want to get a call from me—I always called when she wasn't there.

But it seemed that Asia was doing more than just sitting in the pews. She was listening, learning, and apparently opening her Bible beyond the scriptures that I gave to the congregation every Sunday.

Asia asked, "But why are you telling me this, Aunt Beverly? I'm not mocking God. I don't even really know what that means."

I nodded and waited for a moment, wanting to give her the best answer possible. "It just means that you can't fool God. And you can't turn up your nose or ignore what He wants and what He wants you to do."

In her sigh, I could tell that she still didn't understand. "Sometimes I don't know what God wants from me. I pray, but..." She stopped.

"Well, you know this. You know He wants you to do right and not wrong. And you know the difference." A beat. "You don't have to pray to God and ask Him if you should be involved with Bobby or not. You don't need to ask Him should you sin."

"Aunt..."

I held up my hand, knowing that she was going to say that she didn't want Bobby. But I wasn't going to waste my time with lies when we both knew the truth. I said, "God wants you to know that you will always get back whatever you put out. Yes, you can always go to God for forgiveness. And He will forgive because He is a mighty and just and merciful and wonderful God. But here's the thing..." I stood up and faced all three ladies.

"Here's what you always have to remember. You can always go to God in prayer; He will always meet you there, and He will always forgive you. But know that even forgiven sins have consequences." I let them think about those words and added, "Each one of you is in an interesting situation. And for the most part, you know why you're there, and you know what to do. But you're going to have to pray for strength to do the right thing, pray for answers to your questions, and pray that you will always move forward with wisdom."

I studied their faces as they stared back at me like students in a college lecture hall. They were each calculating my words, adding up how they applied to their lives, their situations.

But that was all they did—just listen. It didn't seem like Sheridan, Kendall, nor Asia had any questions. Which was a good thing because I didn't have anything else to say. My work with these ladies was done...at least for this day.

Well, not everything was done; there was one thing left to do. I reached for Sheridan's hand; she stood and walked toward me. Then we both reached for Kendall and Asia. We formed a circle of four, holding hands, and without me having to say a word, the ladies bowed their heads.

And there in front of the altar, we raised our petitions to God. We prayed our silent prayers.

THE END

COMING JUNE 2014

Forever an Ex

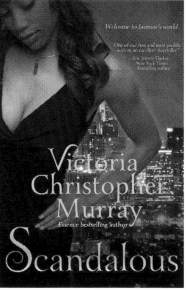
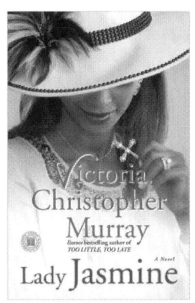
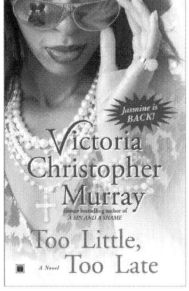

"Once again, Victoria Christopher Murray has crafted a compelling, intriguing, and page-turning story that stays with you long after you've finished the book."
--ReShonda Tate Billingsley, author of *A Family Affair*

"Murray's story has the kind of momentum that prompts you to elbow disbelief aside and flip the pages in horrified enjoyment."
--*The Washington Post*

Victoria Christopher Murray is the *Essence* bestselling author of over 20 novels, including THE DEAL, THE DANCE, AND THE DEVIL; SCANDALOUS; DESTINY'S DIVAS; and NEVER SAY NEVER. She has received numerous awards including the Golden Pen Award for Best Inspirational Fiction and the Phyllis Wheatley Trailblazer Award for being a pioneer in African American Fiction. Since 2007, Victoria has won six African American Literary Awards for best novel, best Christian fiction and Author of the Year - Female. Her 2013 NAACP Image Award nomination for Destiny's Divas was her second Image Award nomination.

Victoria splits her time between Los Angeles and Washington, D.C. You can follow her on Twitter at @VictoriaECM or visit her website at http://www.VictoriaChristopherMurray.com.

Printed in Germany
by Amazon Distribution
GmbH, Leipzig